Slog's
dad

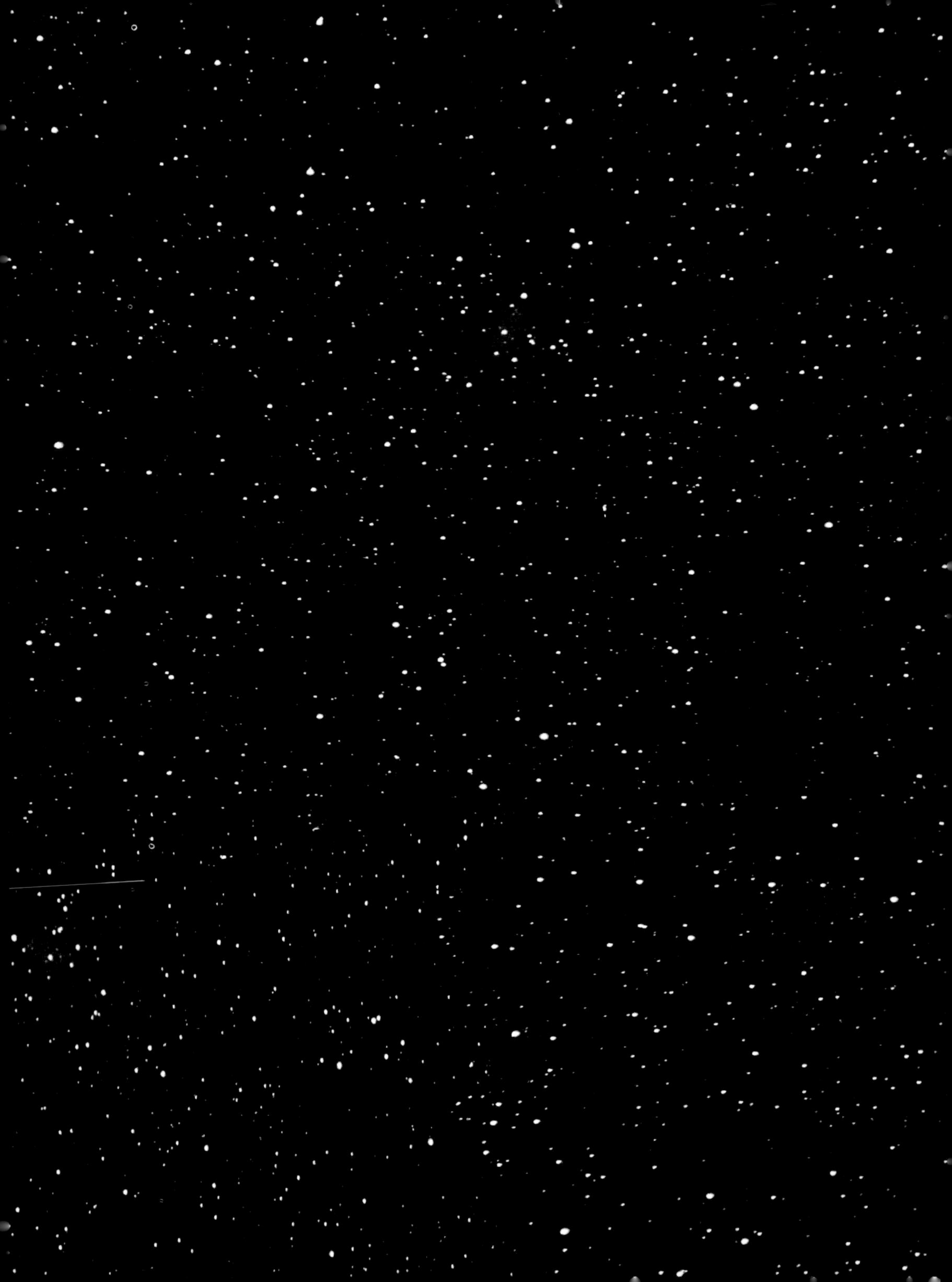

Slog's dad

David Almond

illustrated by

Dave McKean

CANDLEWICK PRESS

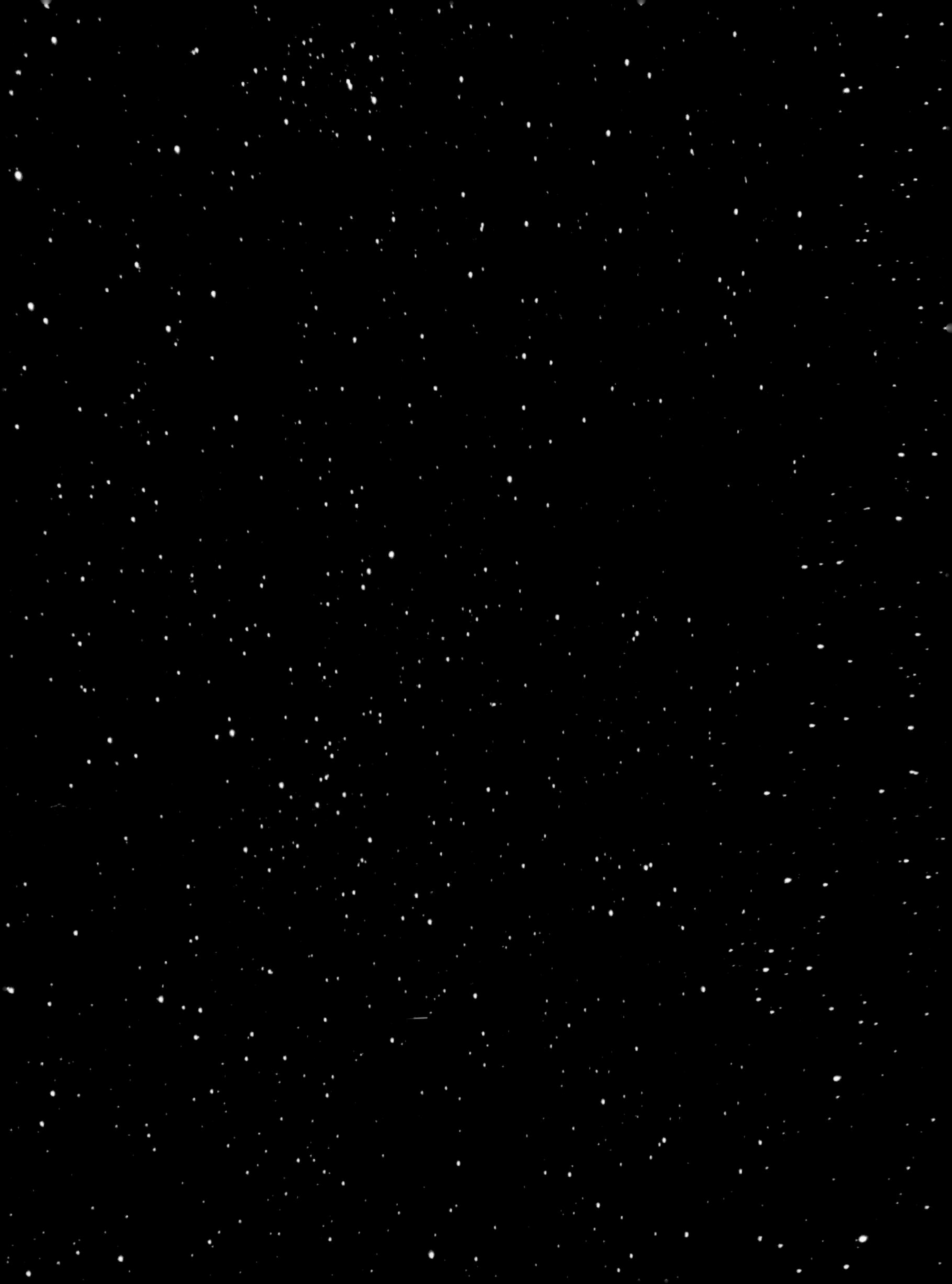

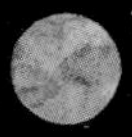

For Paul and Anne Mack

D. A.

This one's for my dad, Fred –
who never came back,
unless you count his
daily visits via my genes
through my hand,
onto the page.

D. M.

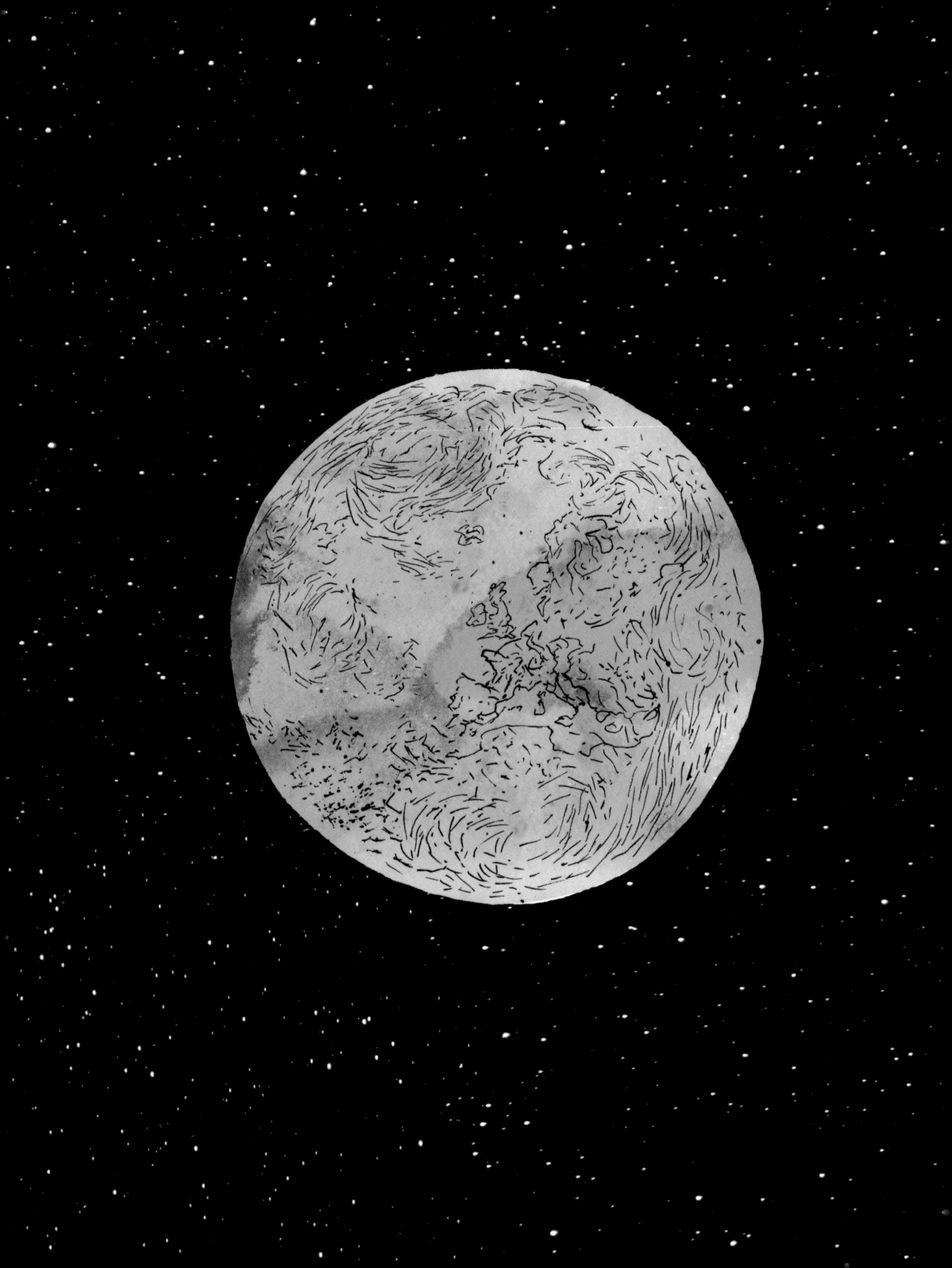

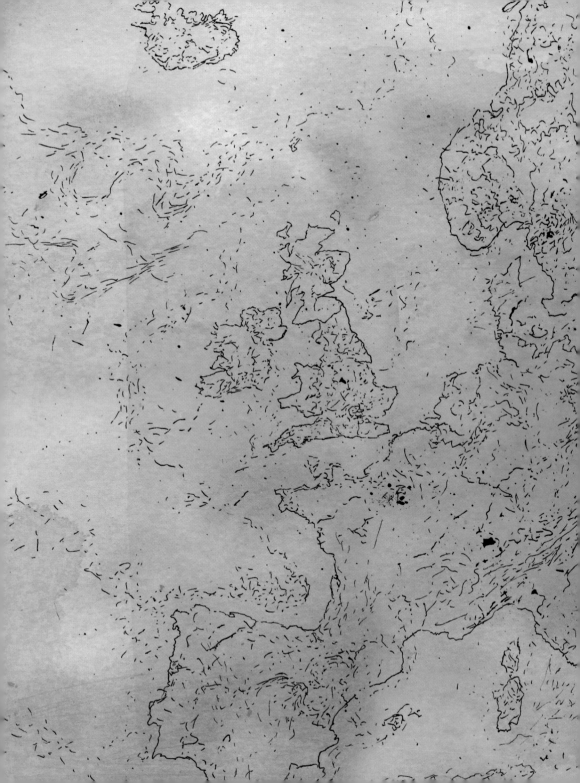

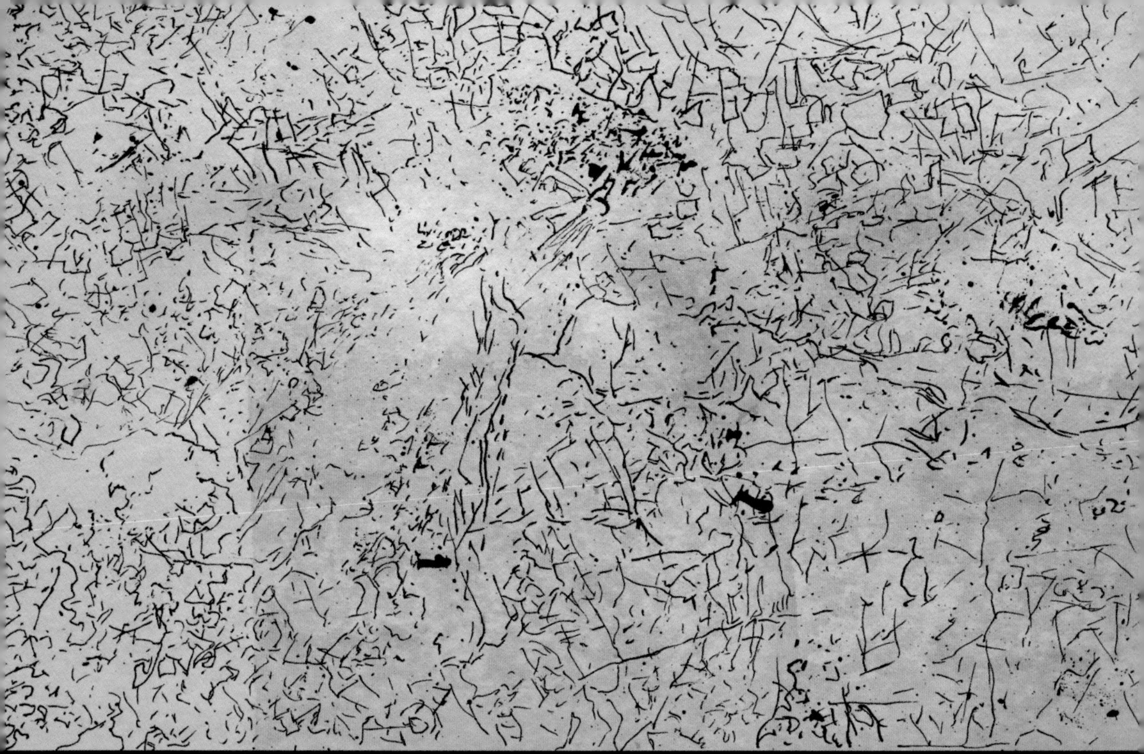
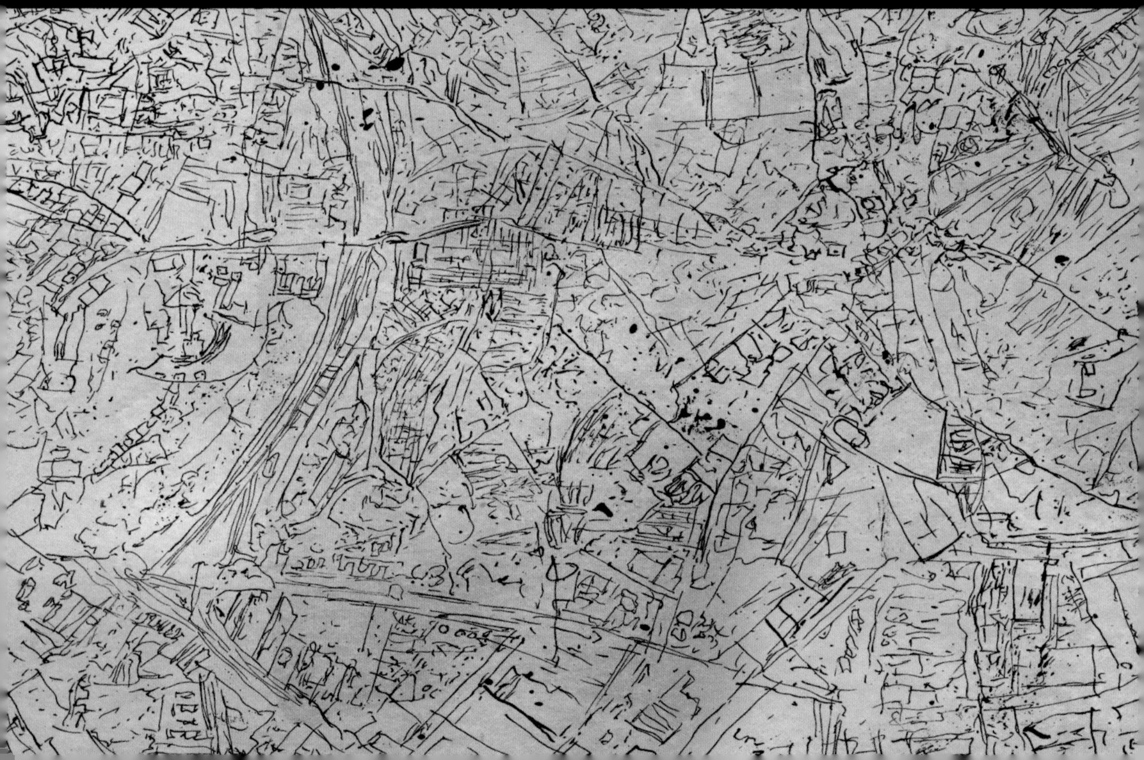

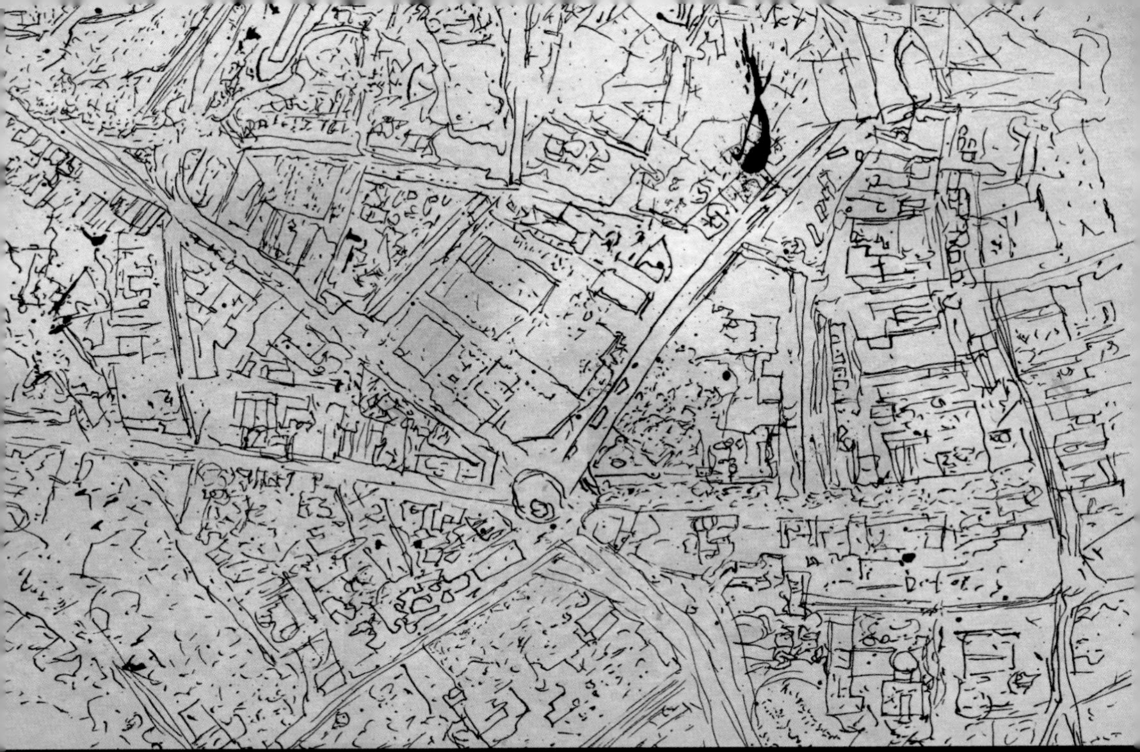

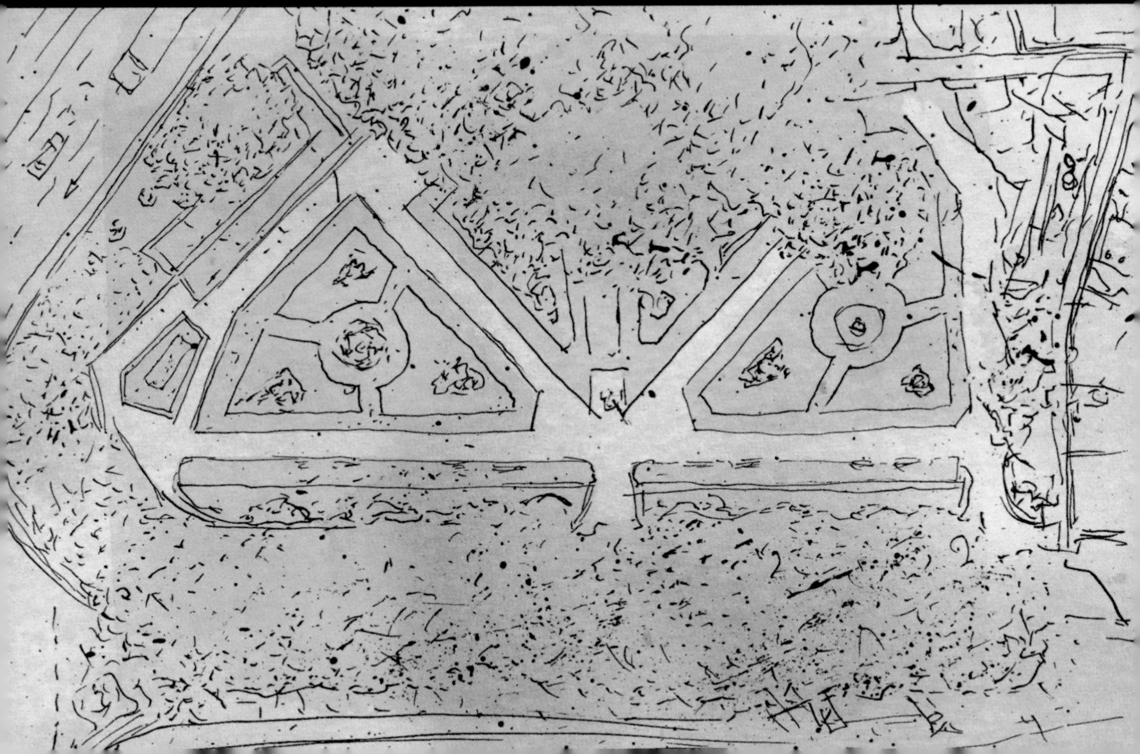

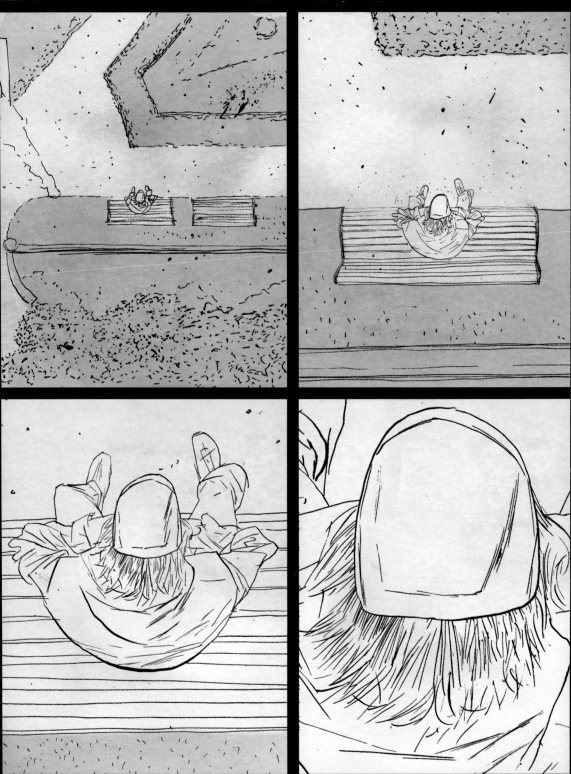

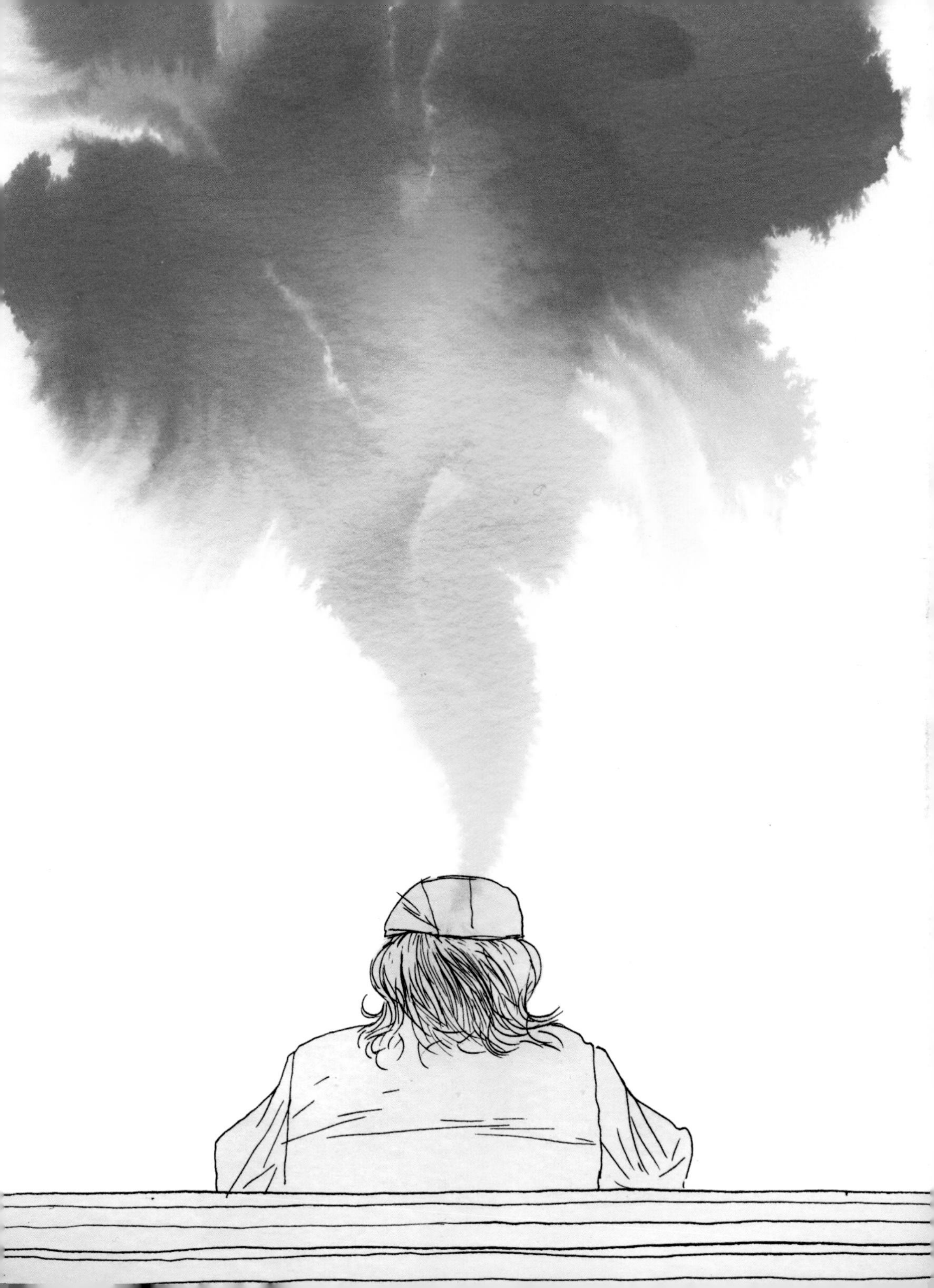

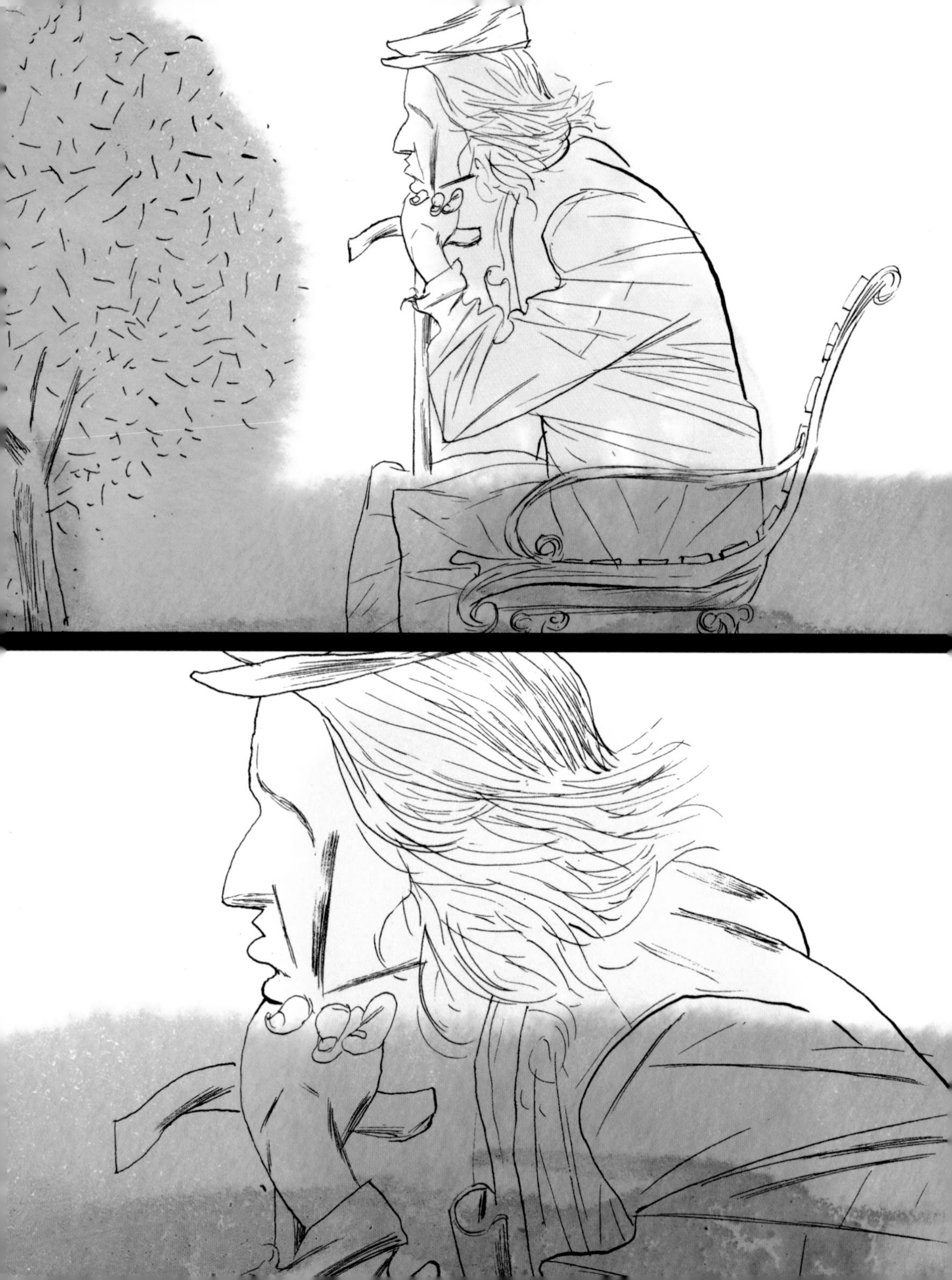

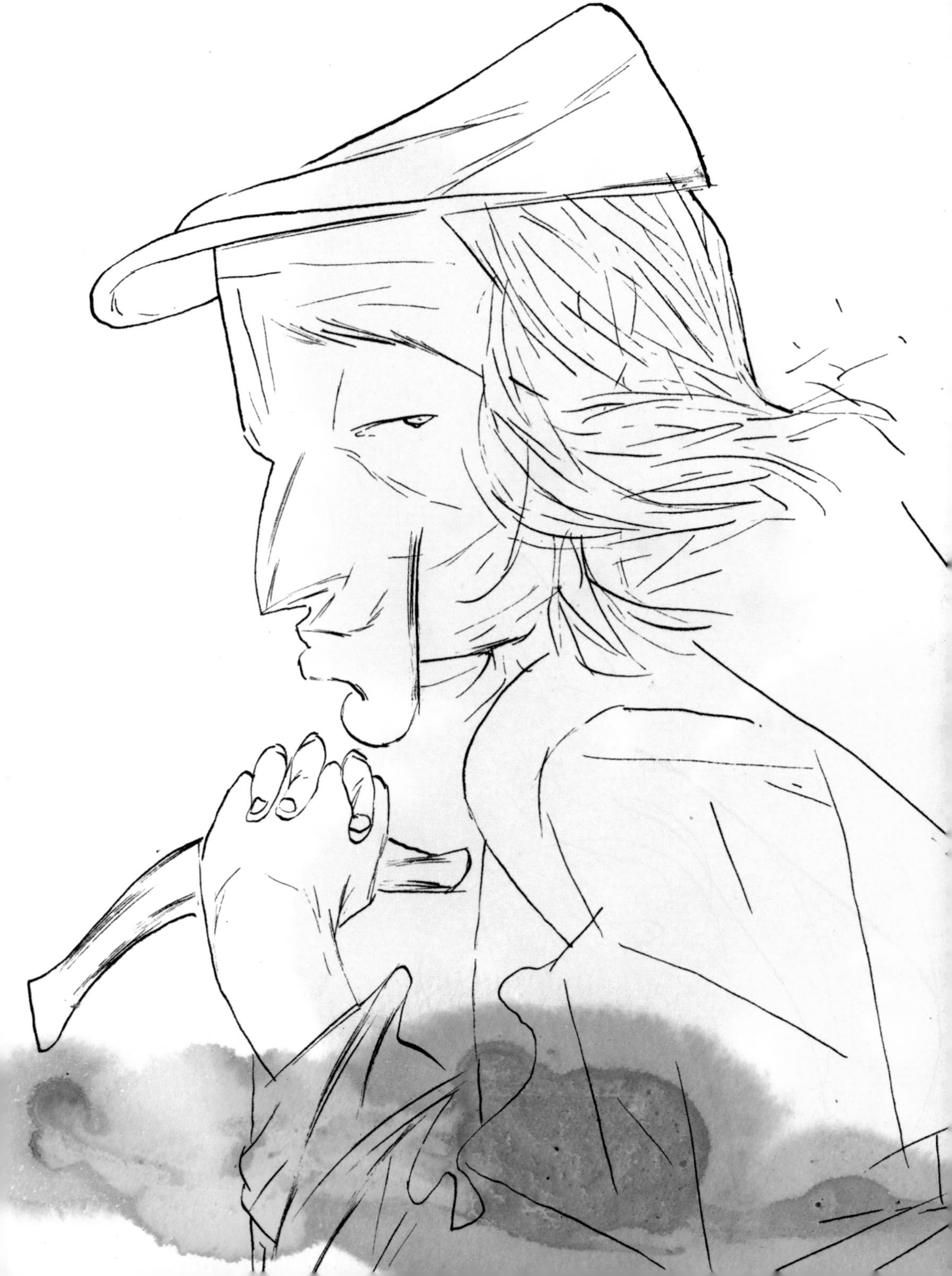

Spring had come. I'd been running round all day with Slog and we were starving. We were crossing the square to Myers' pork shop. Slog stopped dead in his tracks.

"What's up?" I said.

He nodded across the square.

"Look," he said.

"Look at what?"

"It's me dad," he whispered.

"Your dad?"

"Aye."

I just looked at him.

"That bloke there," he said.

"What bloke where?"

"Him on the bench. Him with the cap on. Him with the stick."

I shielded my eyes from the sun with my hand and tried to see. The bloke had his hands resting on the top of the stick. He had his chin resting on his hands. His hair was long and tangled and his clothes were tattered and worn, like he was poor or like he'd been on a long journey. His face was in the shadow of the brim of his cap, but you could see that he was smiling.

"Slogger, man," I said. "Your dad's dead."

"I know that, Davie. But it's him. He's come back again, like he said he would. In the spring."

He raised his arm and waved.

"Dad!" he shouted. "Dad!"

The bloke waved back.

"See?" said Slog. "Howay."

He tugged my arm.

"No," I whispered. "No!"

And I yanked myself free and I went into Myers', and Slog ran across the square to his dad.

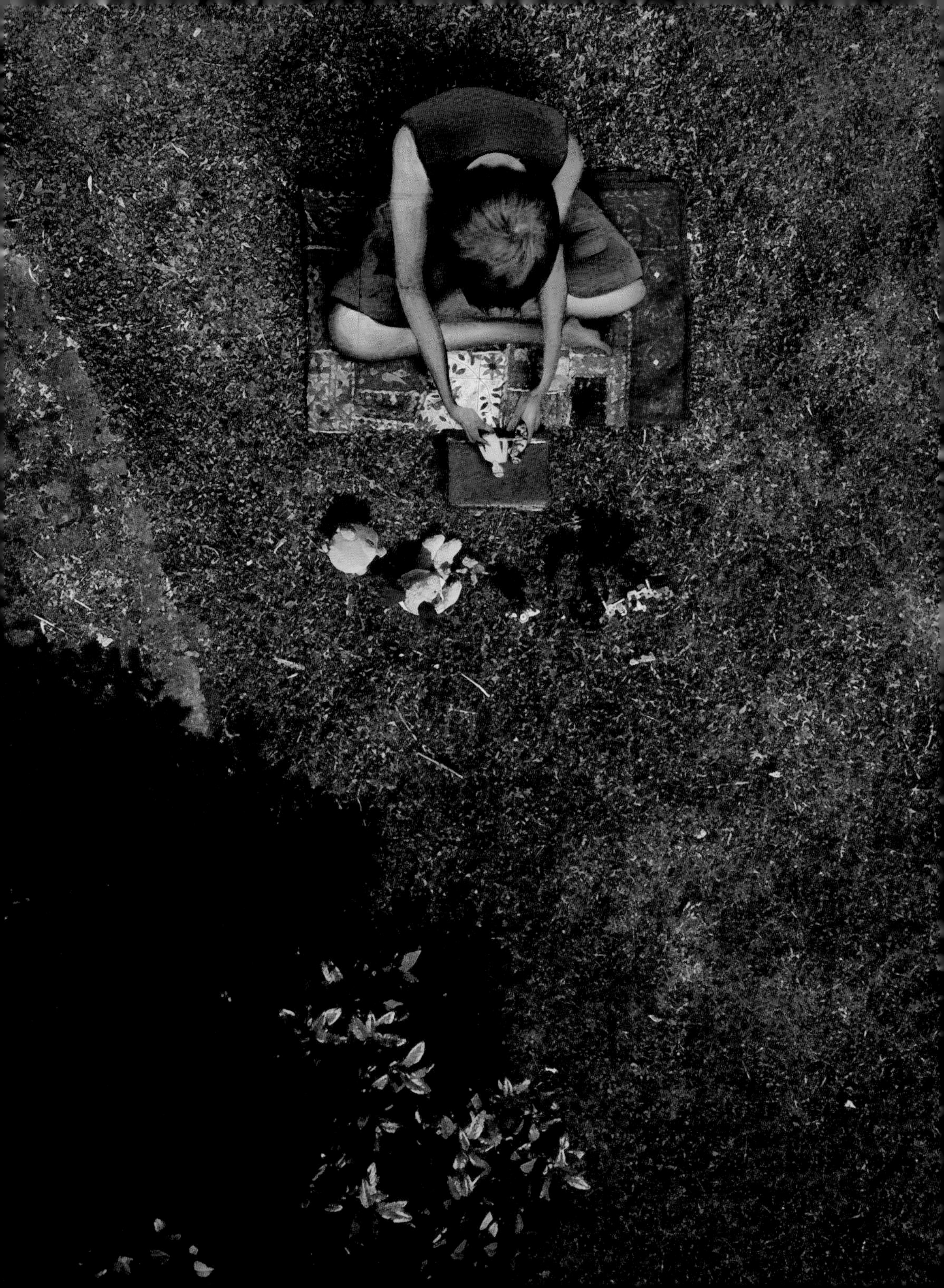

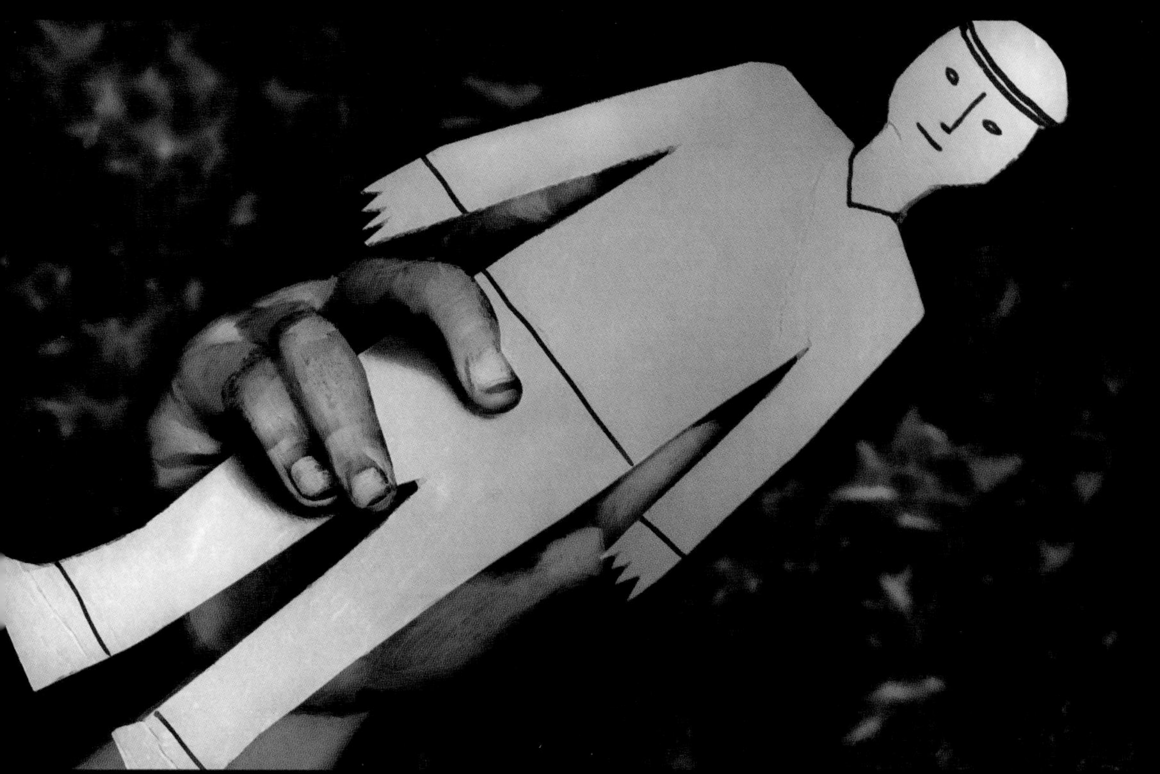
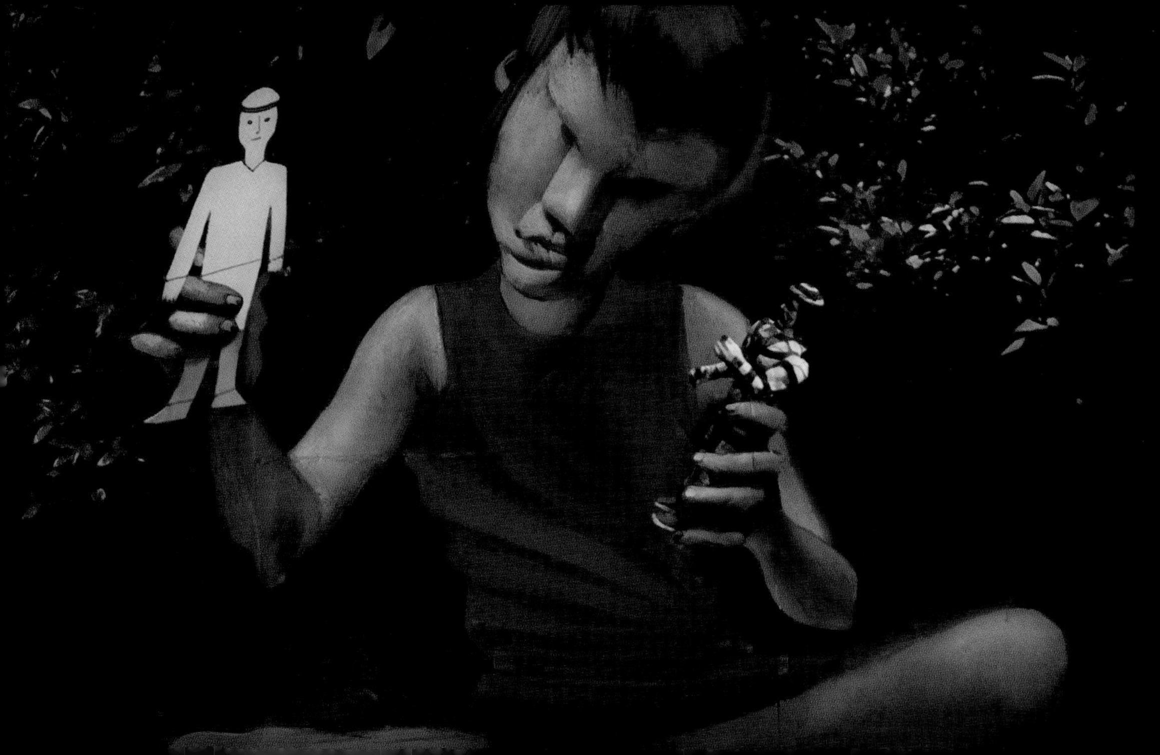

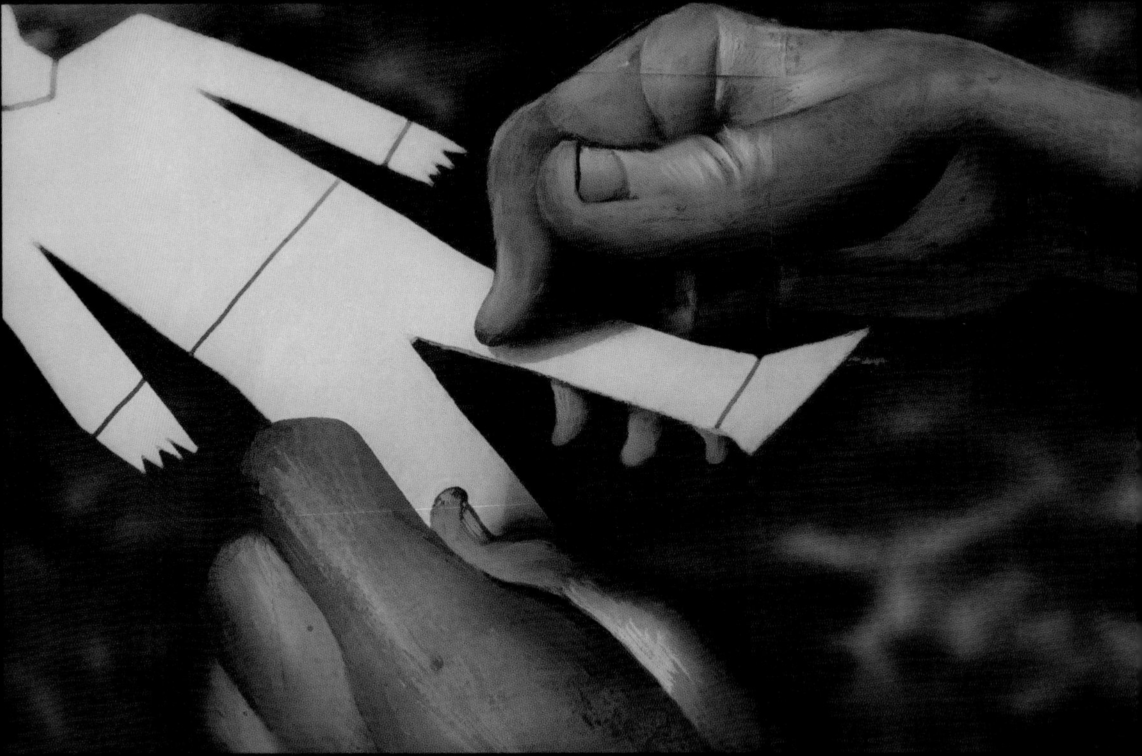

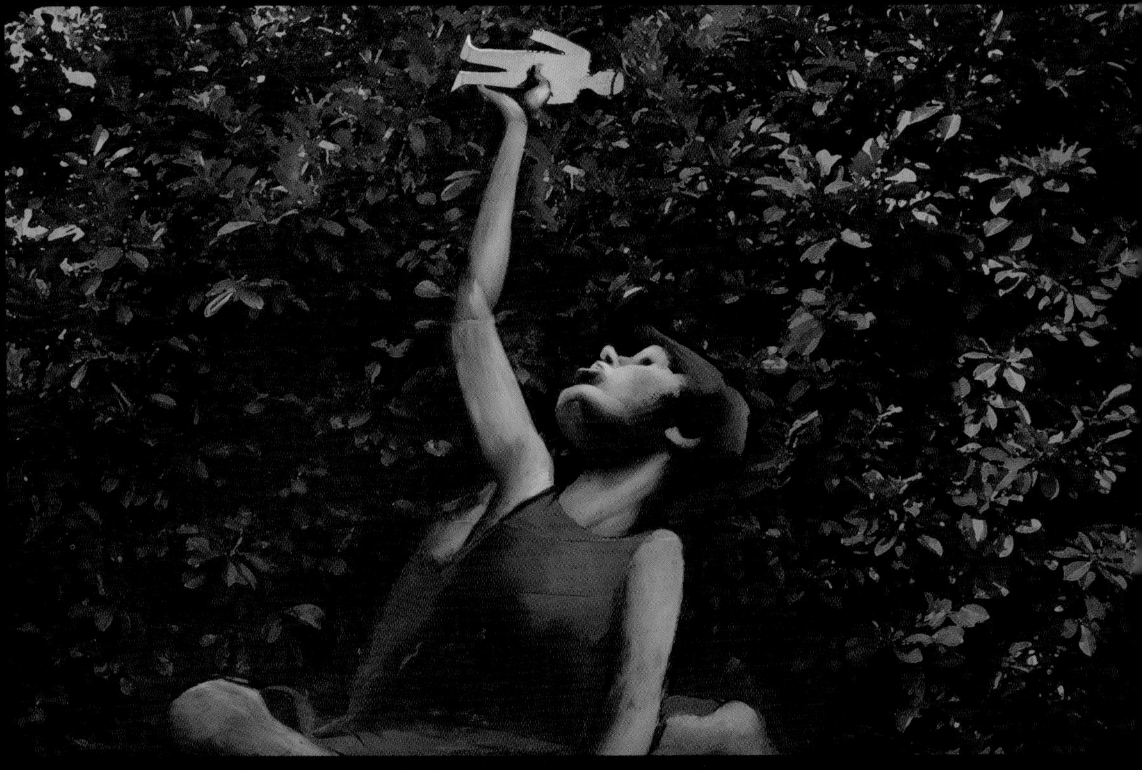

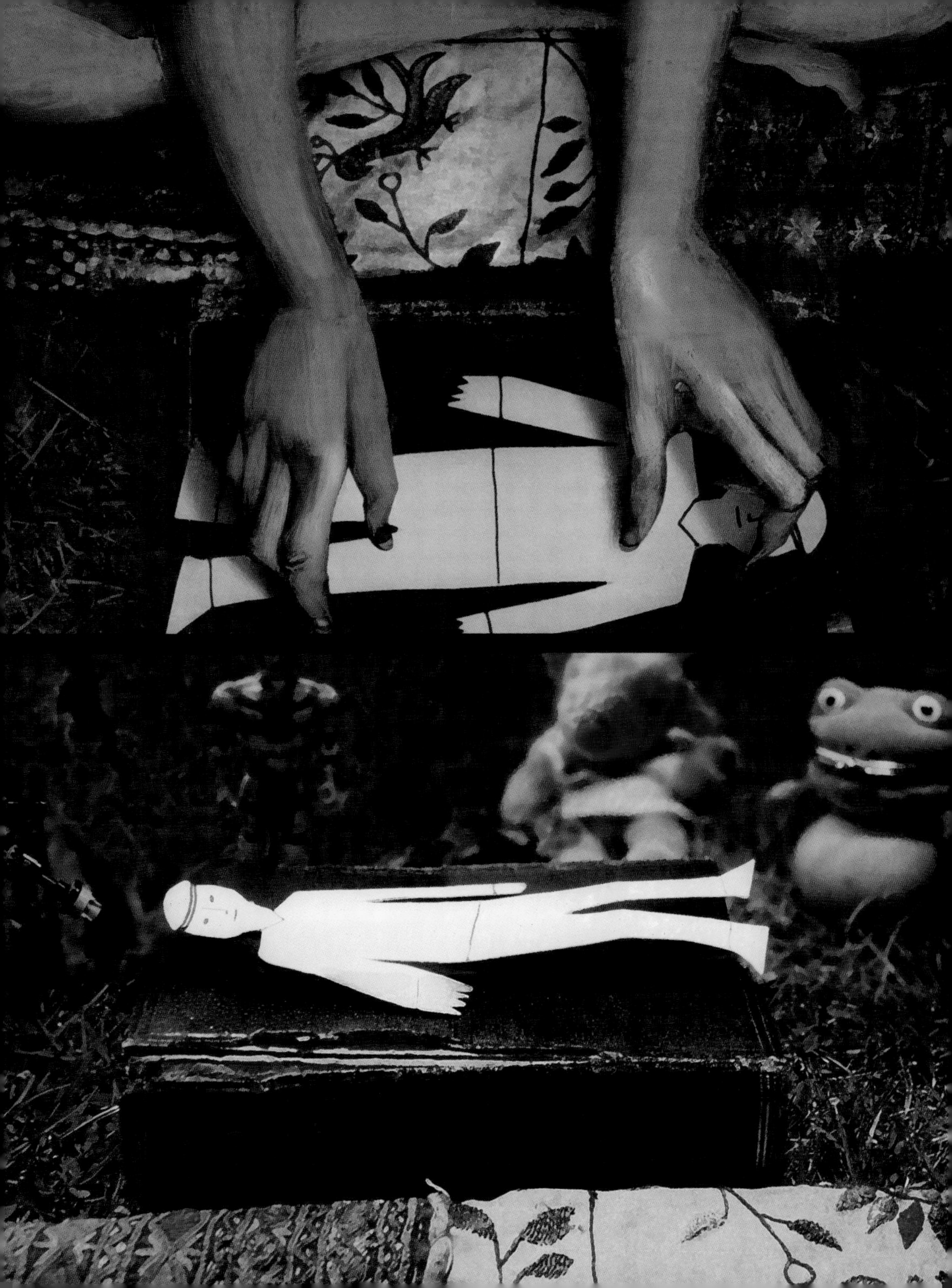

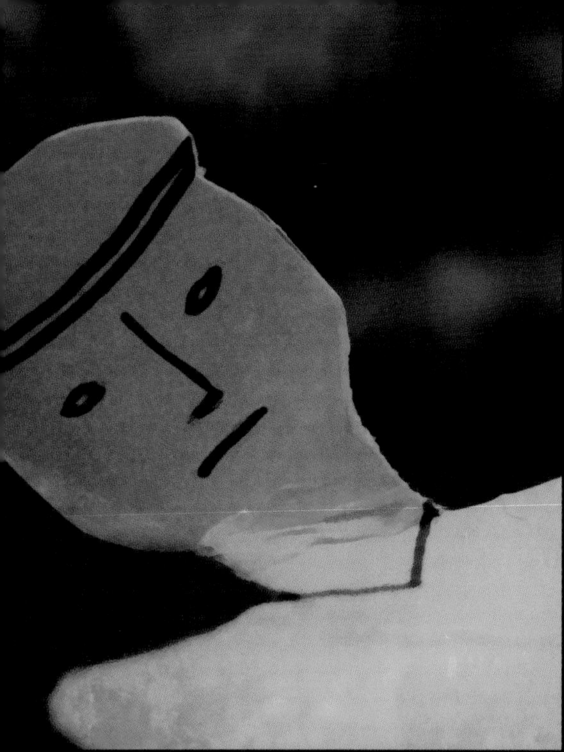
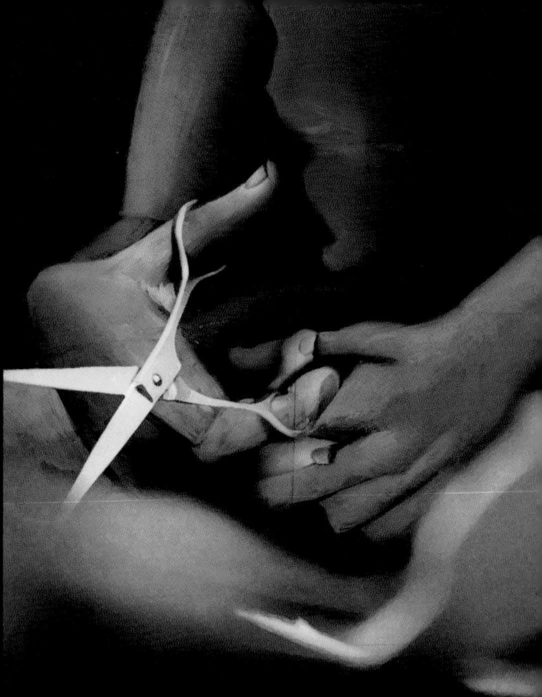
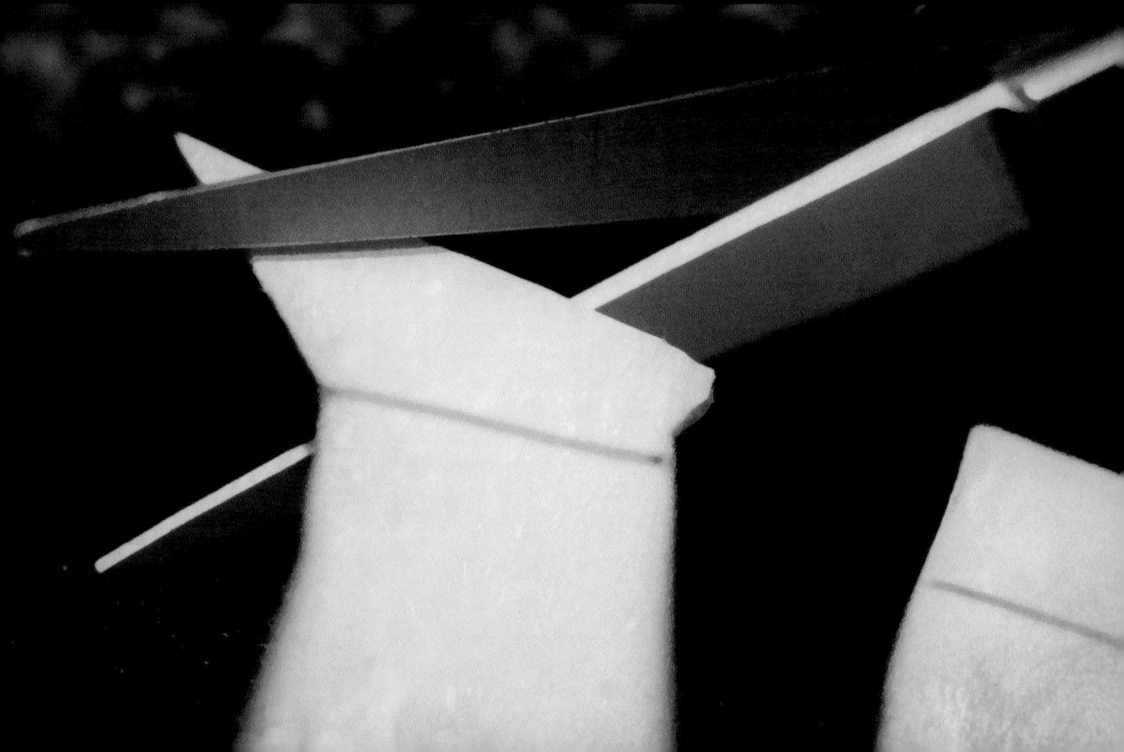

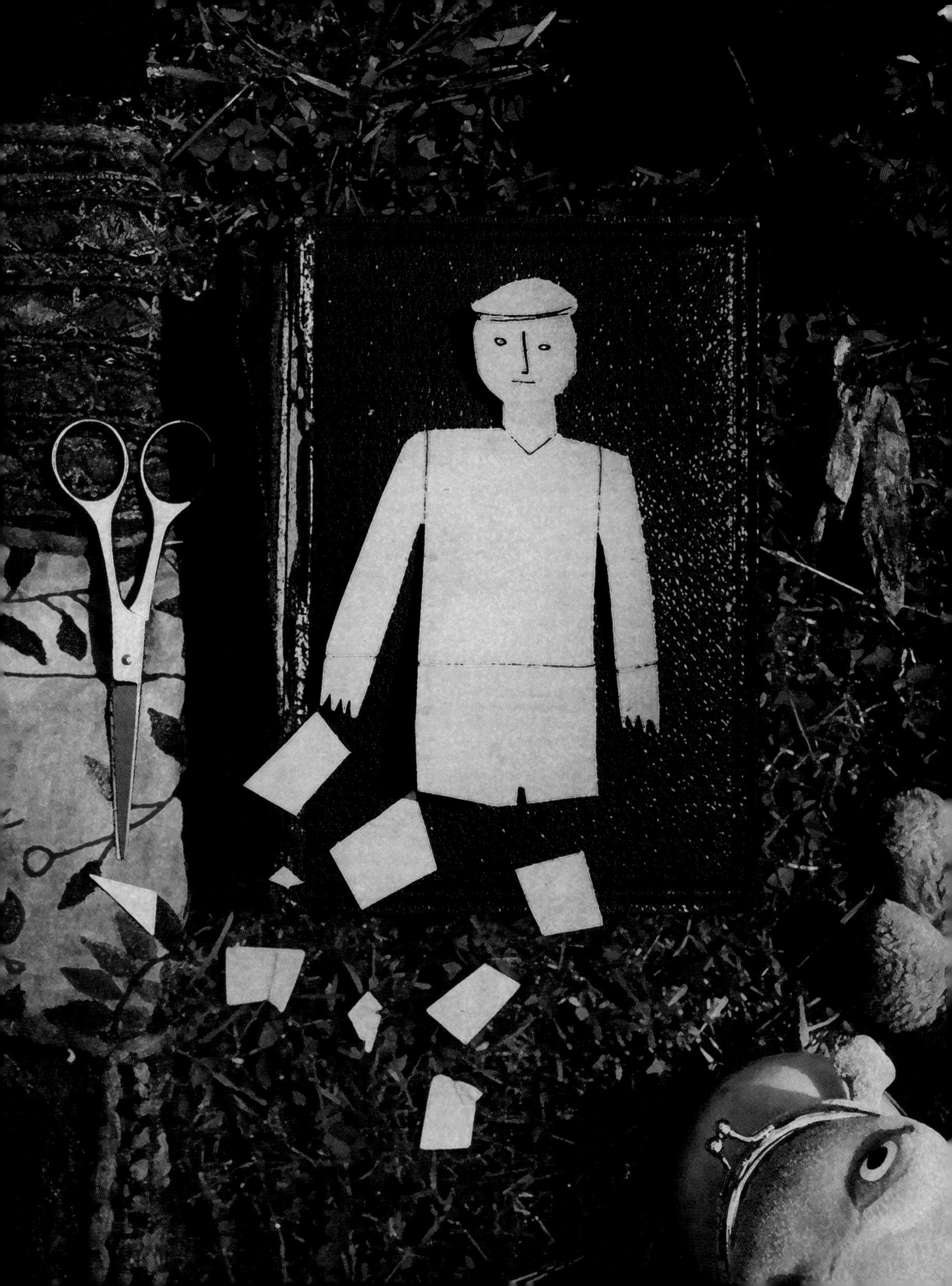

Slog's dad had been a binman, a skinny bloke with a creased face and a greasy flat cap. He was always puffing on a Woodbine. He hung on to the back of the bin wagon as it lurched through the neighborhood, jumped off and on, slung the bins over his shoulder, tipped the muck into the back. He was forever singing hymns—"Faith of Our Fathers," "Hail Glorious Saint Patrick," stuff like that.

"Here he comes again," my mam would say as he bashed the bins and belted out "Oh, Sacred Heart" at eight o'clock on a Thursday morning.

But she'd be smiling, because everybody liked Slog's dad, Joe Mickley, a daft and canny soul.

First sign of his illness was just a bit of a limp; then Slog came to school one day and said, "Me dad's got a black spot on his big toenail."

"Just like *Treasure Island*, eh?" I said.

"What's it mean?" he said.

I was going to say death and doom, but I said, "He could try asking the doctor."

"He has asked the doctor."

Slog looked down. I could smell his dad on him, the scent of rotten rubbish that was always on him. They lived just down the street from us, and the whole house had that smell in it, no matter how much Mrs. Mickley washed and scrubbed. Slog's dad knew it. He said it was the smell of the earth. He said there'd be nowt like it in Heaven.

"The doctor said it's nowt," Slog said. "But he's staying in bed today, and he's going to hospital tomorrow. What's it mean, Davie?"

"How should I know?" I said.

I shrugged.

"It's just a spot, man, Slog!" I said.

Everything happened fast after that. They took the big toe off, then the foot, then the leg to halfway up the thigh. Slog said his mother reckoned his dad had caught some germs from the bins. My mother said it was all the Woodbines he puffed. Whatever it was, it seemed they stopped it. They fitted a tin leg on him and sent him home. It was the end of the bins, of course.

He took to sitting on the little garden wall outside the house. Mrs. Mickley often sat with him and they'd be smelling their roses and nattering and smiling and swigging tea and puffing Woodbines. He used to show off his new leg to passersby.

"I'll get the old one back when I'm in Heaven," he said.

If anybody asked was he looking for work, he'd laugh.

"Work? I can hardly bliddy walk."

And he'd start in on "Faith of Our Fathers" and everybody'd smile.

Then he got a black spot on his other big toenail, and they took him away again, and they started chopping at his other leg, and Slog said it was like living in a horror picture.

When Slog's dad came home next, he spent his days parked in a wheelchair in his garden. He didn't bother with tin legs: just pyjama bottoms folded over his stumps. He was quieter. He sat day after day in the summer sun among his roses, staring out at the pebble-dashed walls and the red roofs and the empty sky. The Woodbines dangled in his fingers; "Oh, Sacred Heart" drifted gently from his lips. Mrs. Mickley brought him cups of tea, glasses of beer, Woodbines. Once I stood with Mam at the window and watched Mrs. Mickley stroke her husband's head and gently kiss his cheek.

"She's telling him he's going to get better," said Mam.

We saw the smile growing on Joe Mickley's face.

"That's love," said Mam. "True love."

Slog's dad still joked and called out to anybody passing by.

"Walk?" he'd say. "Man, I cannot even bliddy hop."

"They can hack your body to a hundred bits," he'd say. "But they cannot hack your soul."

We saw him shrinking. Slog told me he'd heard his mother whispering about his dad's fingers coming off. He told me about Mrs. Mickley lifting his dad from the chair each night, laying him down, whispering her good-nights, like he was a little bairn. Slog said that some nights when he was really scared, he got into bed beside them.

"But it just makes it worse," he said. He cried. "I'm bigger than me dad, Davie. I'm bigger than me bliddy dad!"

And he put his arms around me and put his head on my shoulder and cried.

"Slog, man," I said as I tugged away. "Howay, Slogger, man!"

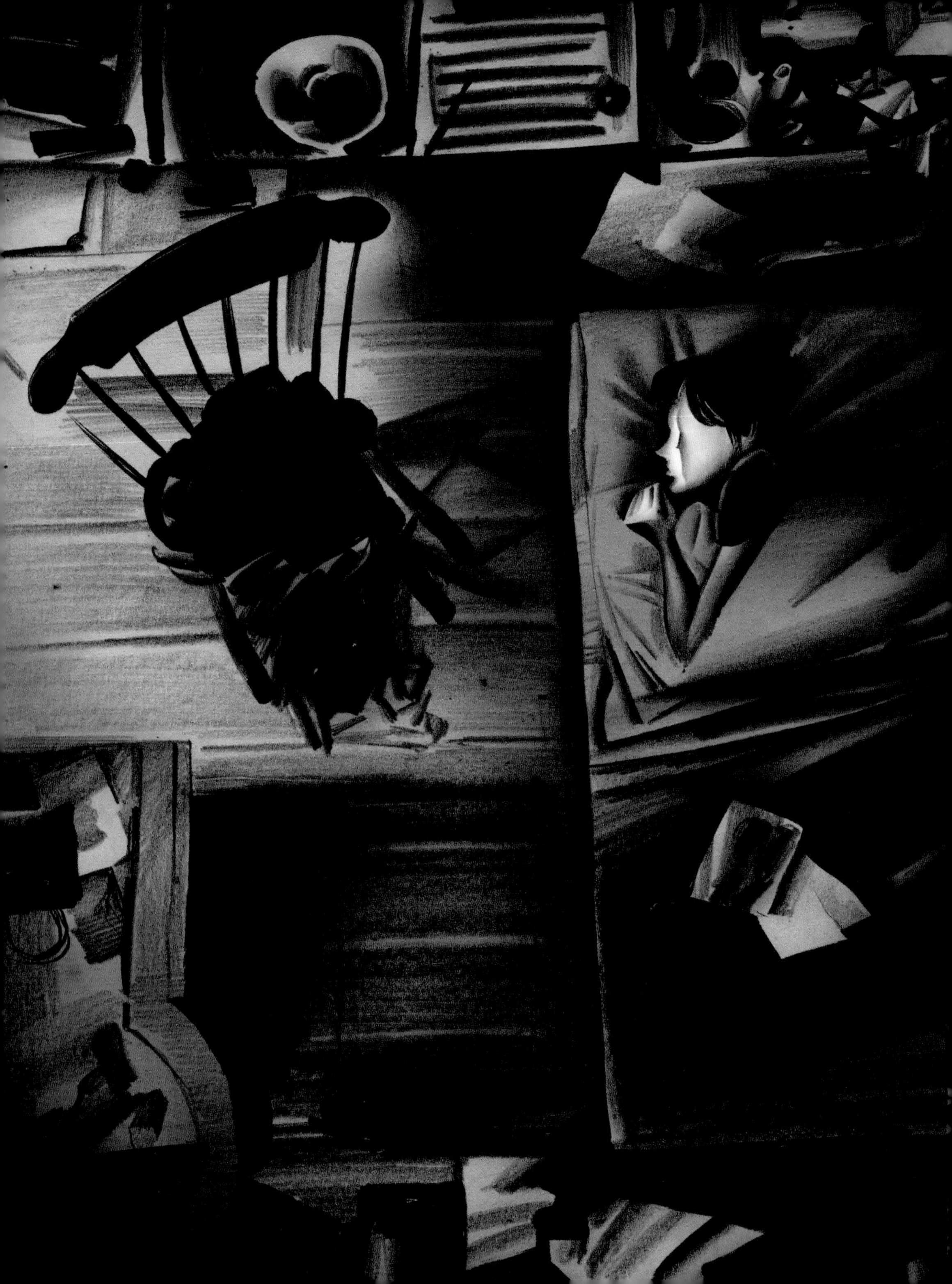

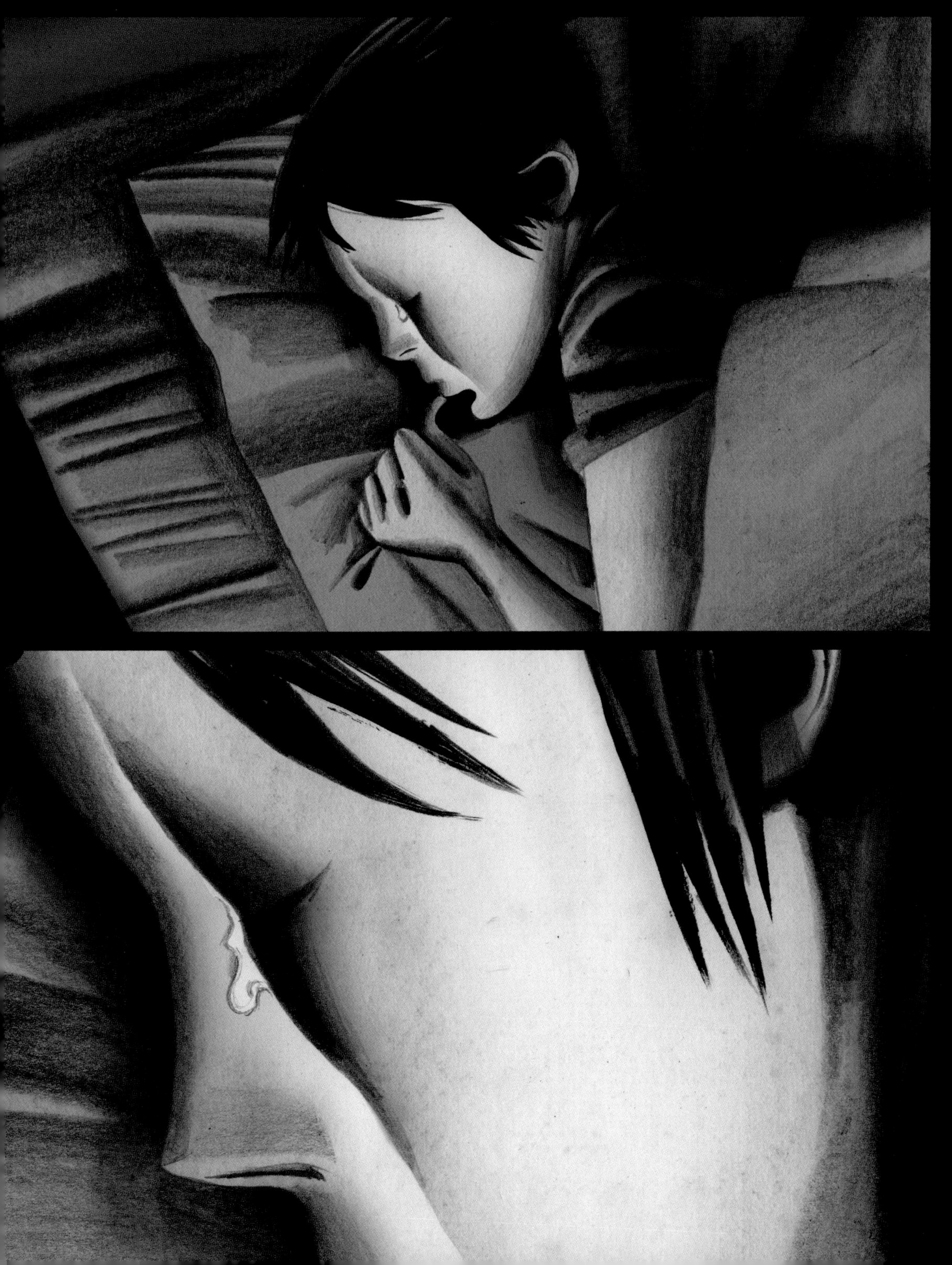

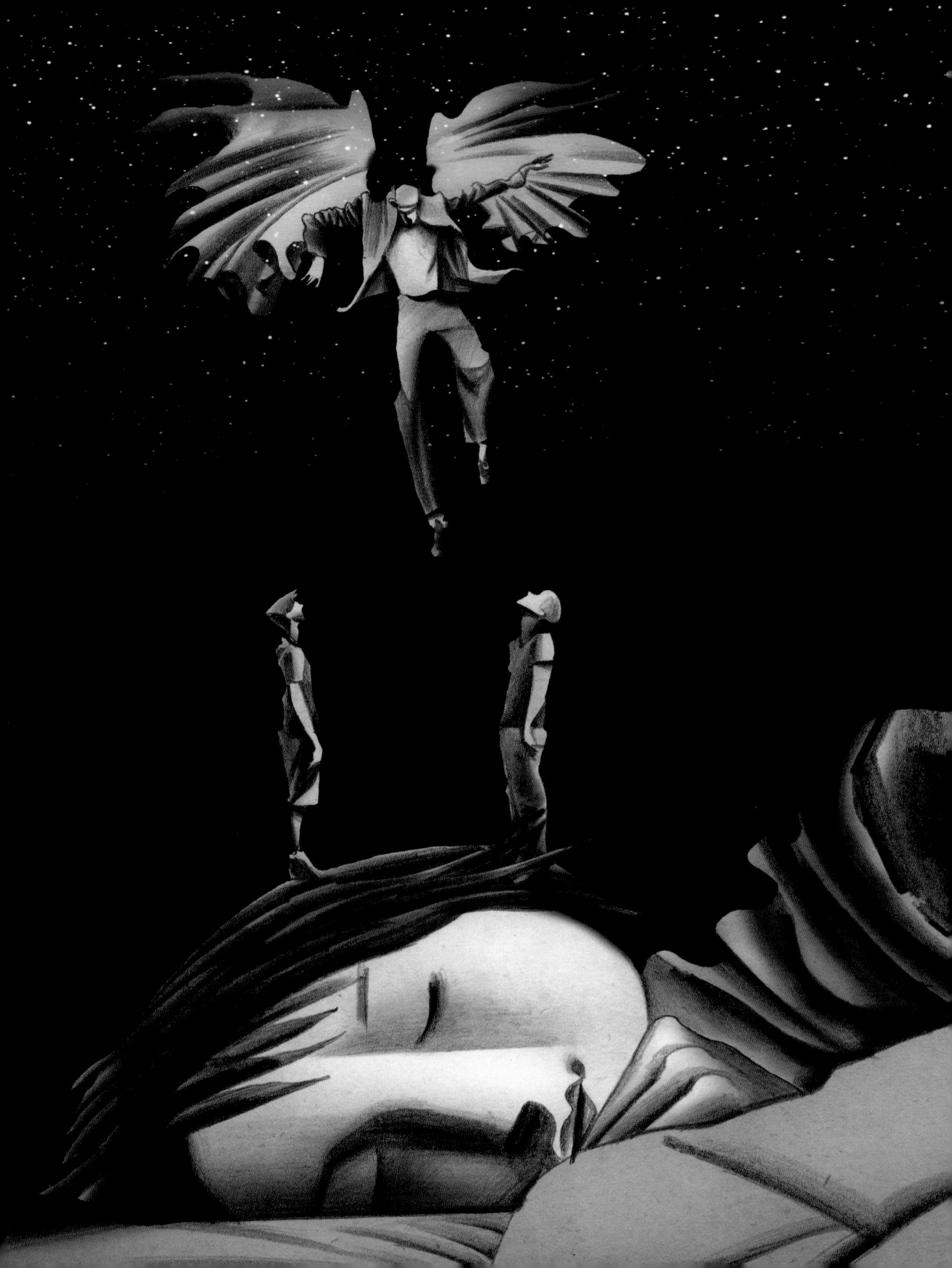

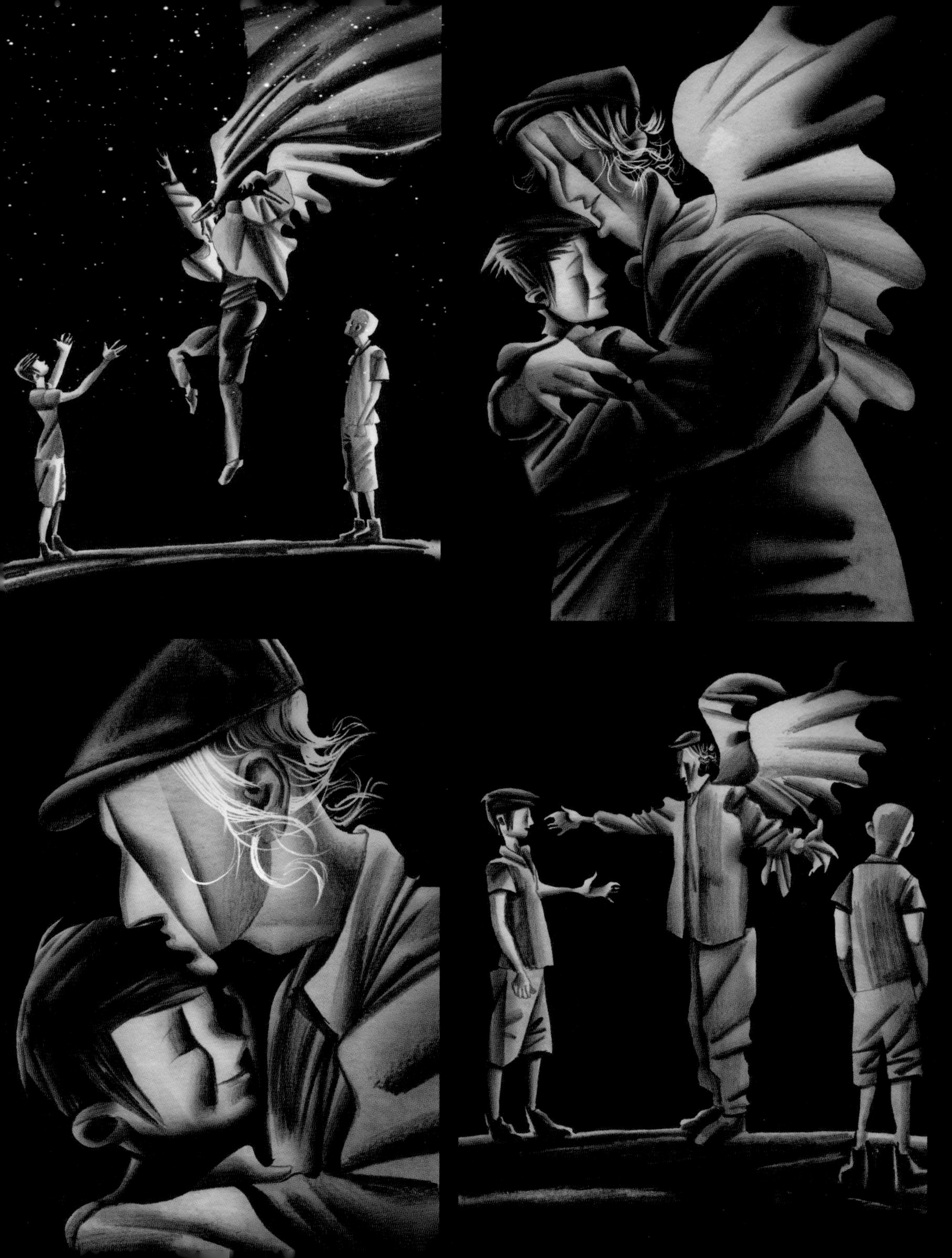

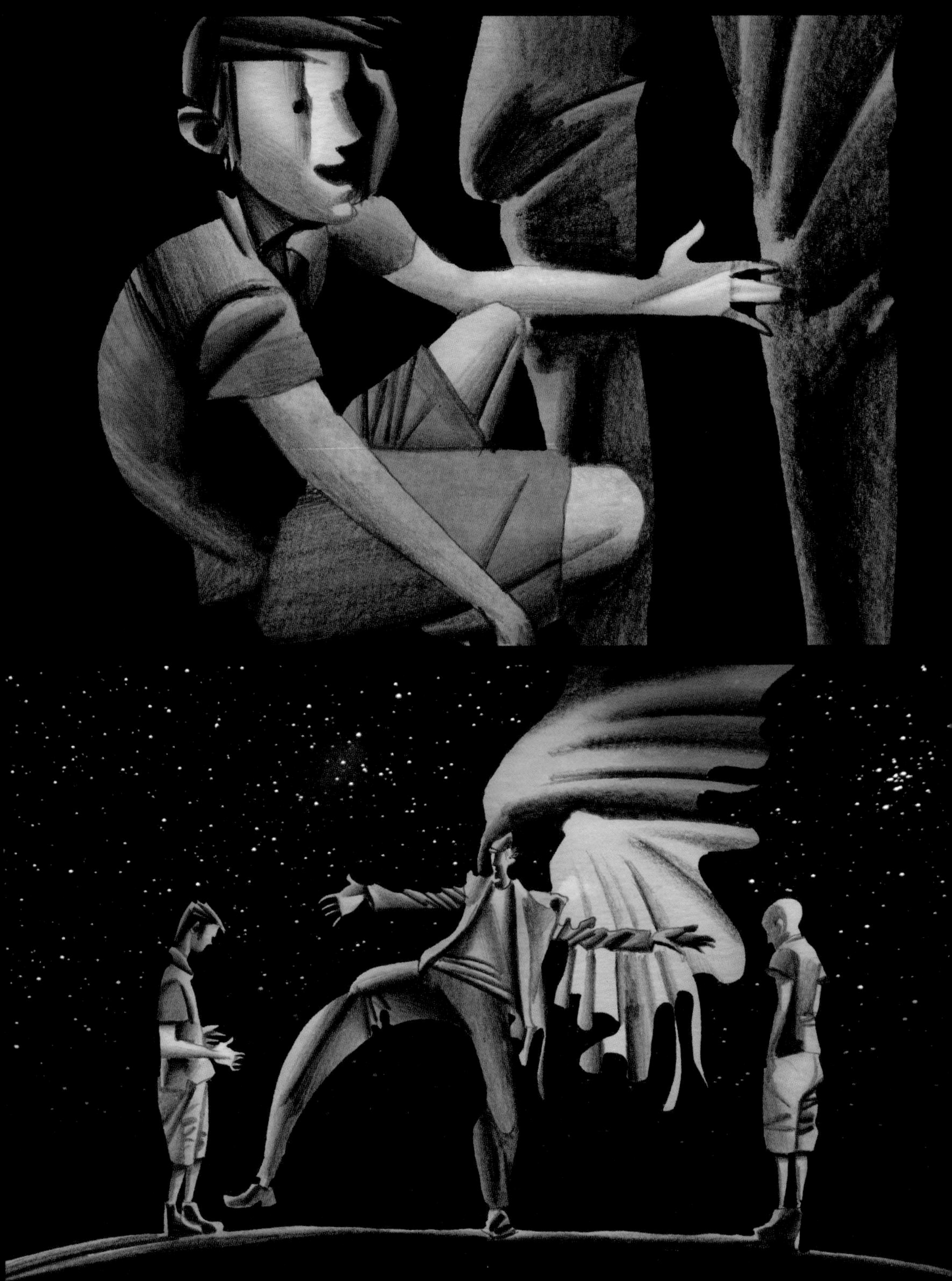

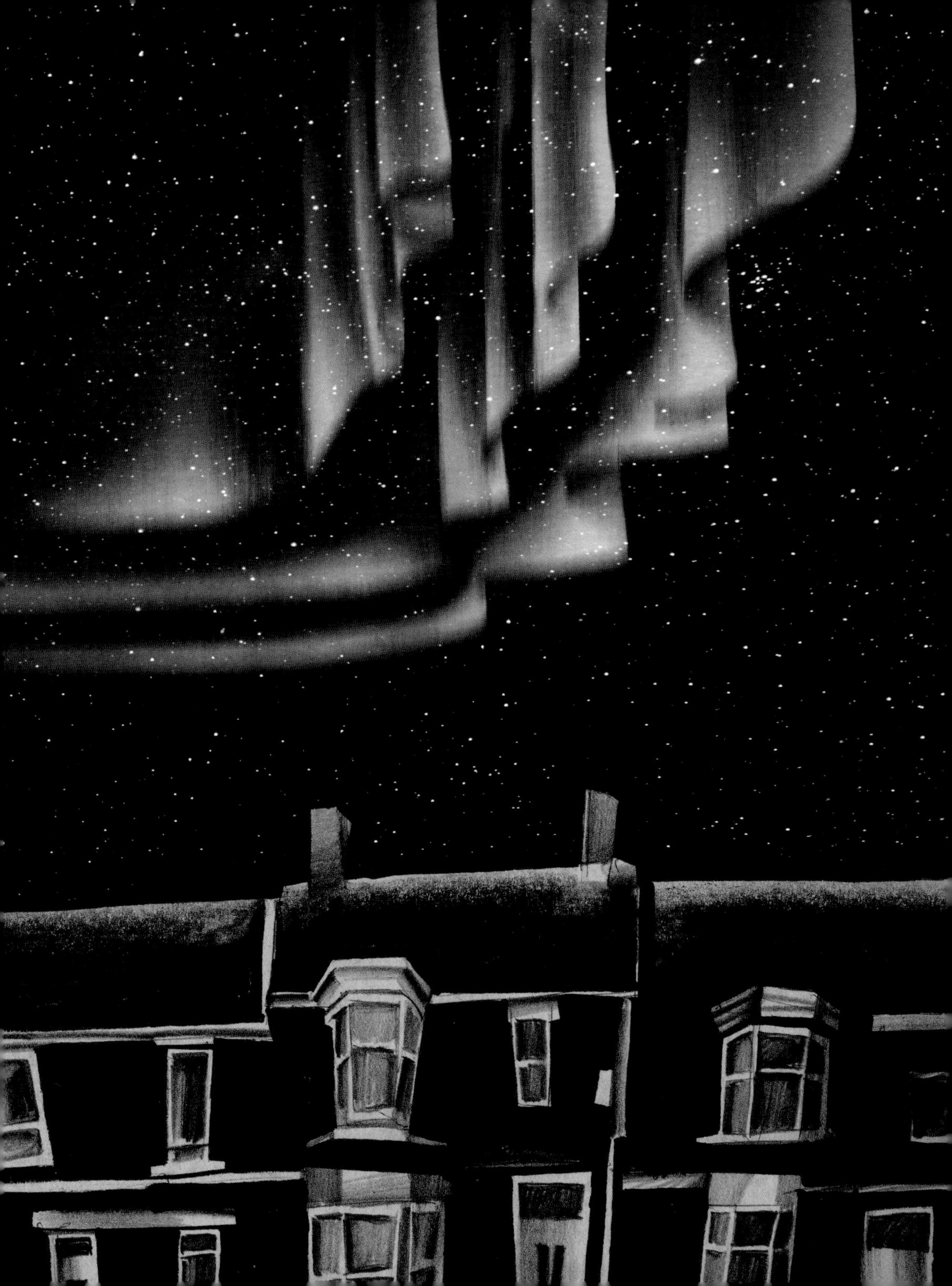

One day late in August, Slog's dad caught me looking. He waved me to him. I went to him slowly. He winked.

"It's alreet," he whispered. "I know you divent want to come too close."

He looked down to where his legs should be.

"They tell us if I get to Heaven, I'll get them back again," he said. "What d'you think of that, Davie?"

I shrugged.

"Dunno, Mr. Mickley," I said.

"Do you reckon I'll be able to walk back here if I do get them back again?"

"Dunno, Mr. Mickley."

I started to back away.

"I'll walk straight out them pearly gates," he said. He laughed. "I'll follow the smells. There's no smells in Heaven. I'll follow the bliddy smells right back here to the lovely earth."

He looked at me.

"What d'you think of that?" he said.

Just a week later, the garden was empty. We saw Dr. Molly going in, then Father O'Mahoney, and just as dusk was coming on, Mr. Blenkinsop, the undertaker.

The week after the funeral, I was heading out to school with Slog, and he told me, "Dad said he's coming back."

"Slogger, man," I said.

"His last words to me. Watch for me in the spring, he said."

"Slogger, man. It's just cos he was . . ."

"What?"

I gritted my teeth.

"Dying, man!"

I didn't mean to yell at him, but the traffic was thundering past us on the bypass. I got hold of his arm and we stopped.

"Bliddy dying," I said more softly.

"Me mam says that and all," said Slog. "She says we'll have to wait. But I cannot wait till I'm in Heaven, Davie. I want to see him here one more time."

Then he stared up at the sky.

"Dad," he whispered. "Dad!"

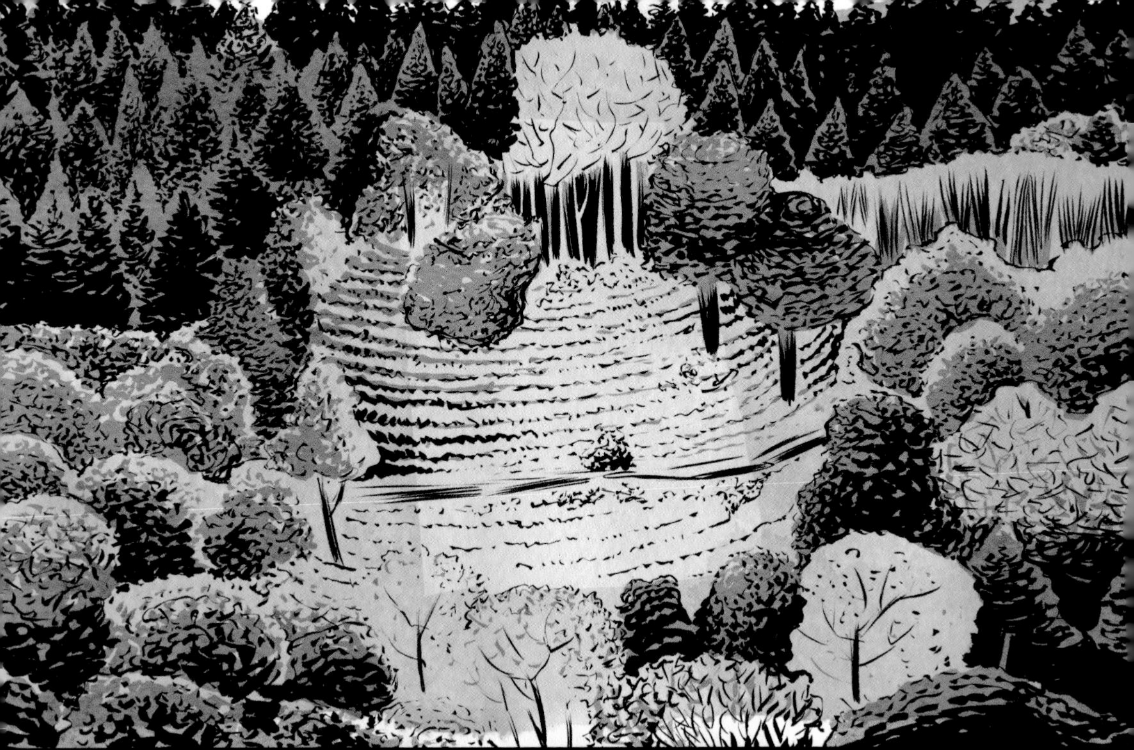
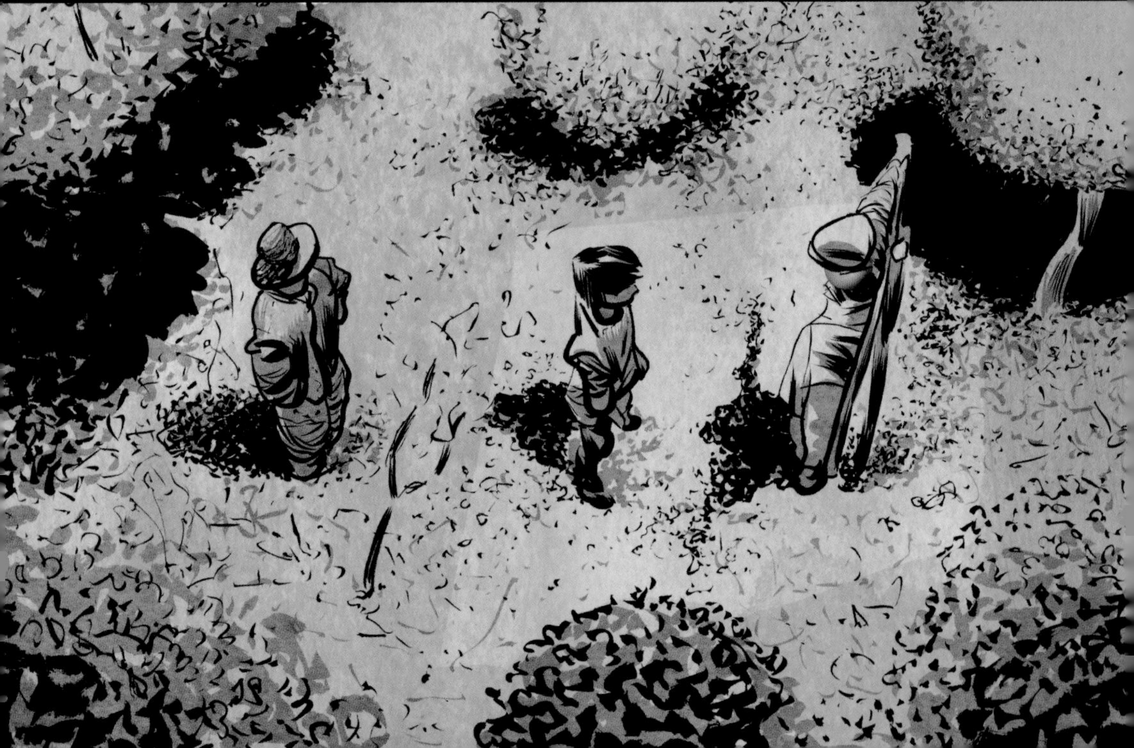

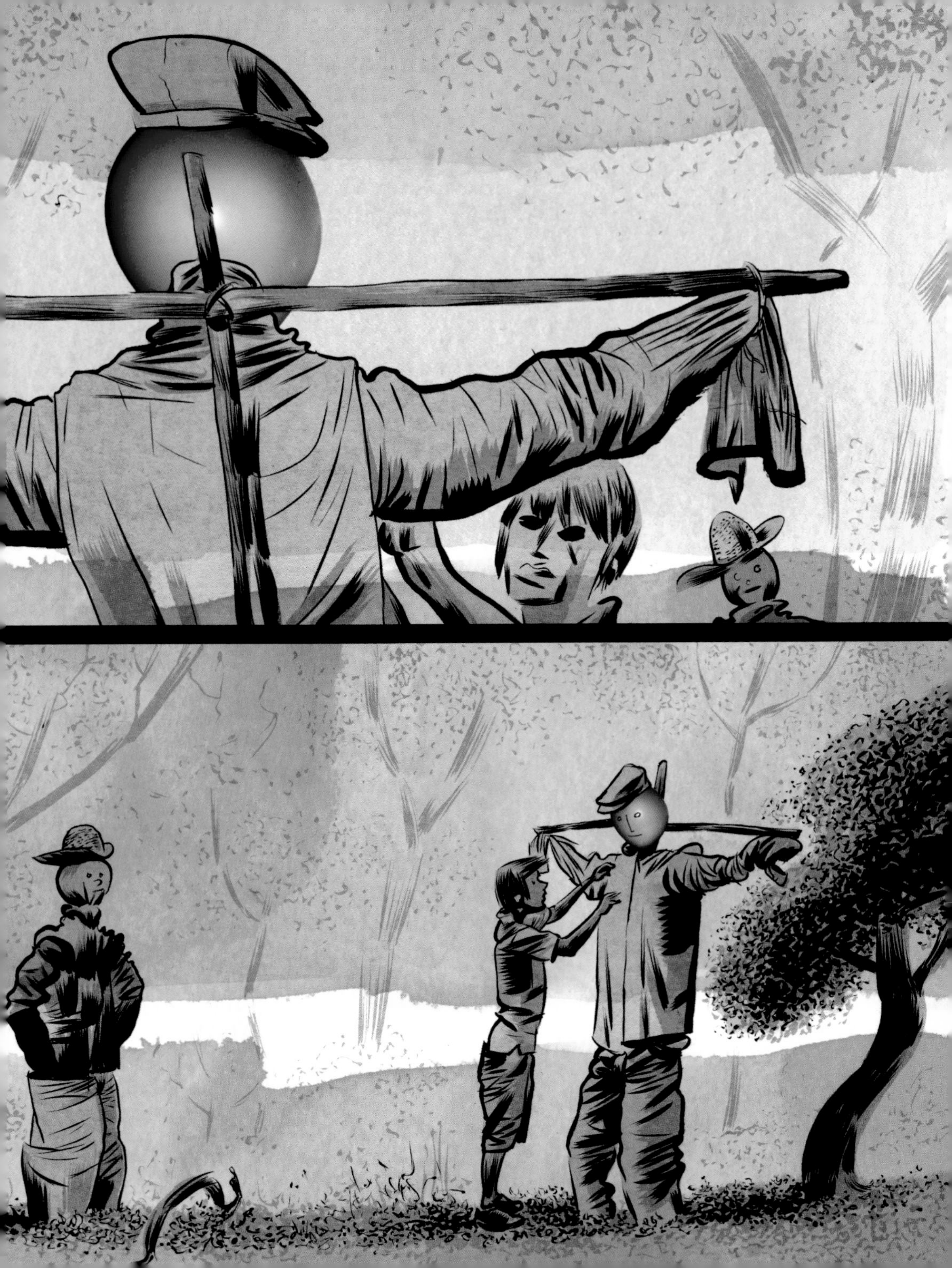

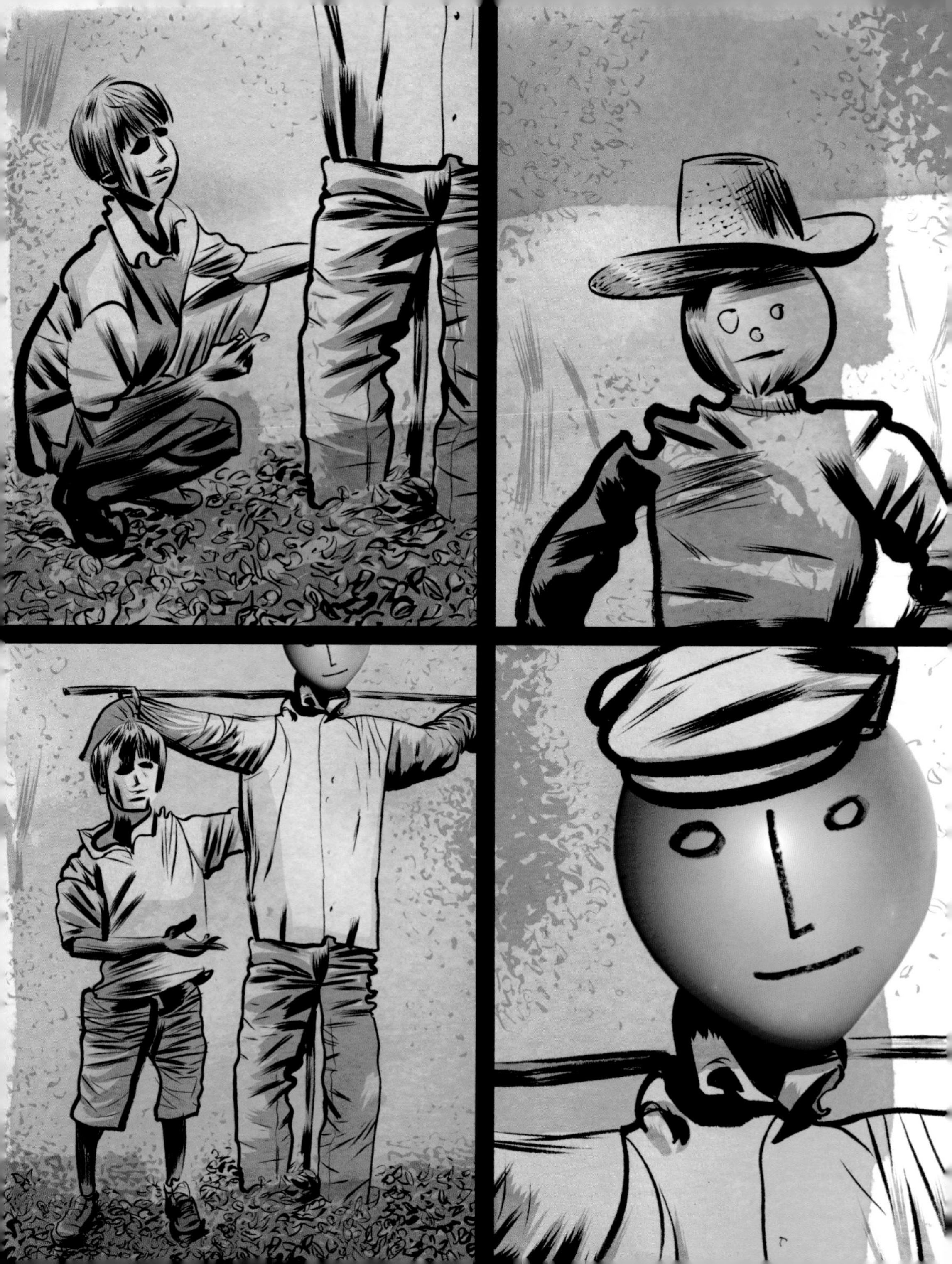

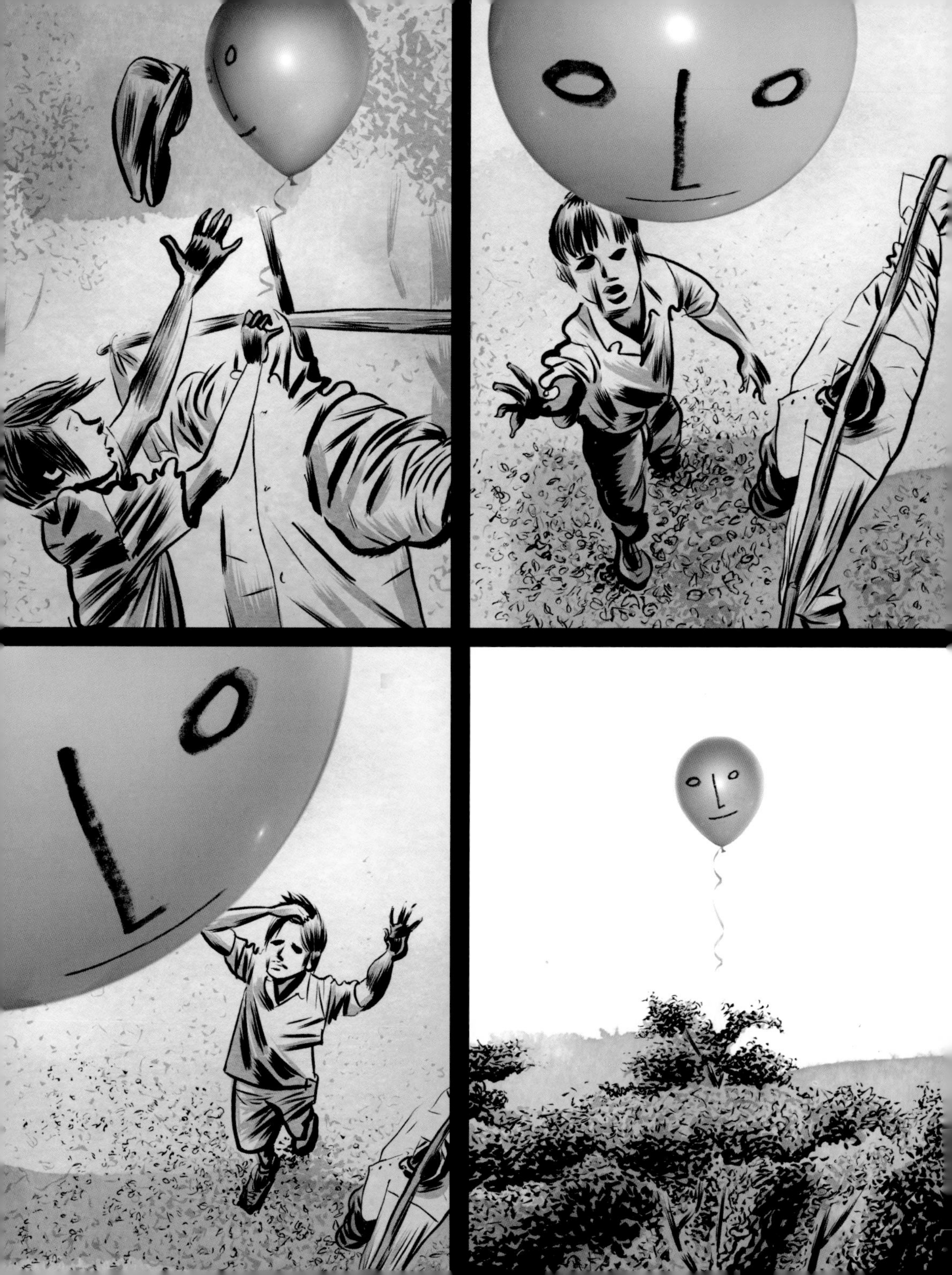

I got into Myers'. Chops and sausages and bacon and black pudding and joints and pies sat in neat piles in the window. A pink pig's head with its hair scorched off and a grin on its face gazed out at the square. There was a bucket of bones for dogs and a bucket of blood on the floor. The marble counters and Billy Myers' face were gleaming.

"Aye-aye, Davie," he said.

"Aye," I muttered.

"Saveloy, I suppose? With everything?"

"Aye. Aye."

I looked out over the pig's head. Slog was with the bloke, looking down at him, talking to him. I saw him lean down to touch the bloke.

"And a dip?" said Billy.

"Aye," I said.

He plunged the sandwich into a trough of gravy.

"Bliddy lovely," he said. "Though I say it myself. A shilling to you, sir."

I paid him but I couldn't go out through the door. The sandwich was hot. The gravy was dripping to my feet.

Billy laughed.

"Penny for them," he said.

I watched Slog get onto the bench beside the bloke.

"Do you believe there's life after death?" I said.

Billy laughed.

"Now there's a question for a butcher!" he said.

A skinny old woman came in past me.

"What can I do you for, pet?" said Billy. "See you, Davie."

He laughed.

"Kids!" he said.

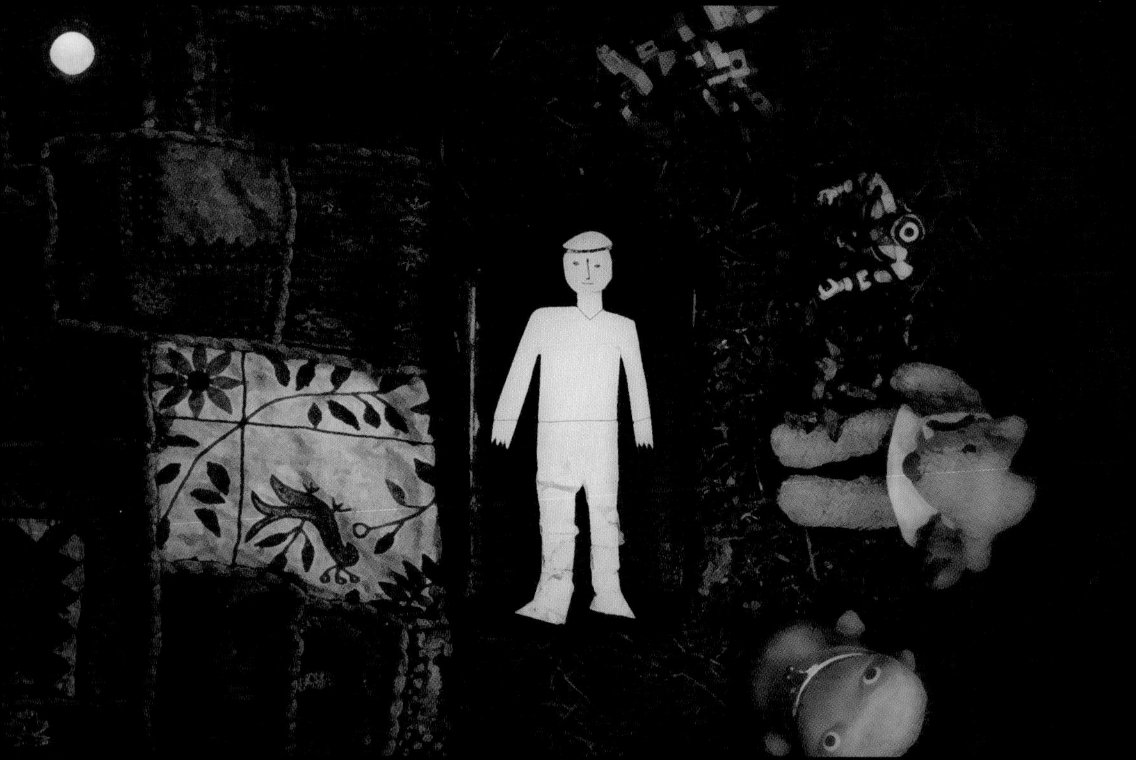

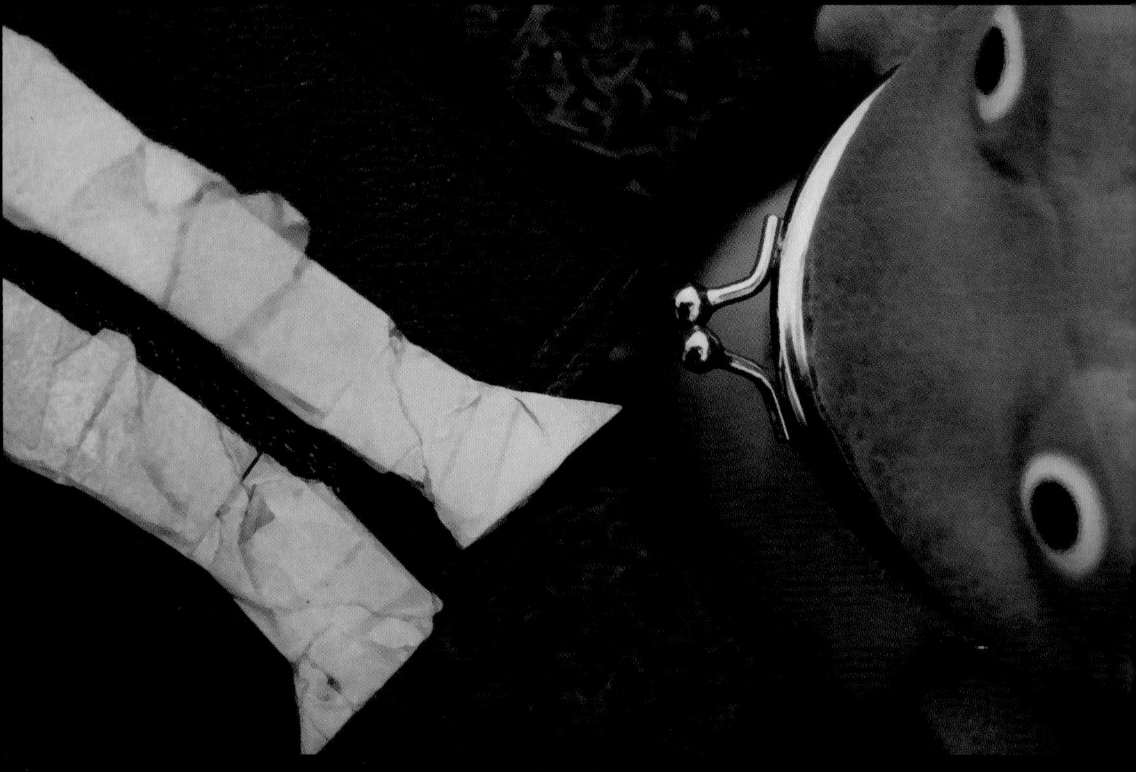

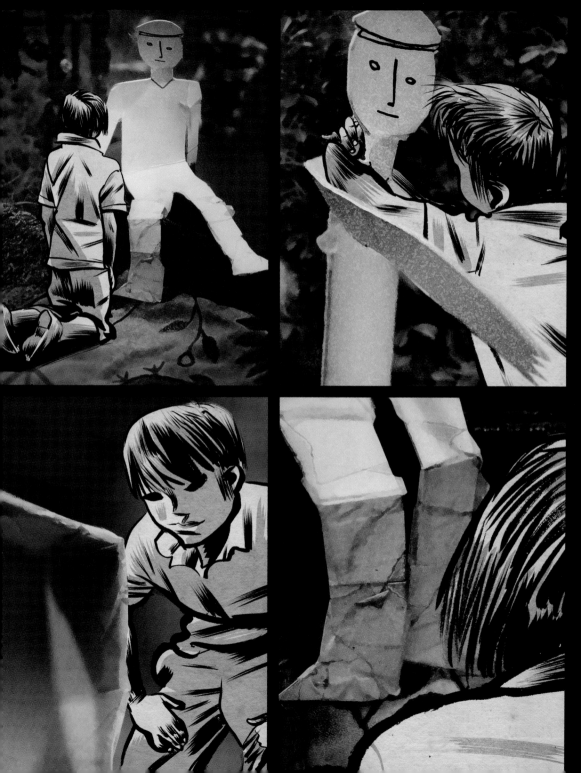

Slog looked that happy as I walked toward them. He was leaning on the bloke and the bloke was leaning back on the bench grinning at the sky. Slog made a fist and face of joy when he saw me.

"It's Dad, Davie!" he said. "See? I told you."

I stood in front of them.

"You remember Davie, Dad," said Slog.

The bloke looked at me. He looked nothing like the Joe Mickley I used to know. His face was filthy but it was smooth and his eyes were shining bright.

"'Course I do," he said. "Nice to see you, son."

Slog laughed.

"Davie's a bit scared," he said.

"No wonder," said the bloke. "That looks very tasty."

I held the sandwich out to him.

He took it, opened it, and smelt it and looked at the meat and pease pudding and stuffing and mustard and gravy. He closed his eyes and smiled, then lifted it to his mouth.

"Saveloy with everything," he said. He licked the gravy from his lips, wiped his chin with his hand. "Bliddy lovely. You got owt to drink?"

"No," I said.

"Ha. He has got a tongue!"

"He looks a bit different," said Slog. "But that's just cos he's been . . ."

"Transfigured," said the bloke.

"Aye," said Slog. "Transfigured. Can I show him your legs, Dad?"

The bloke laughed gently. He bit his saveloy sandwich. His eyes glittered as he watched me.

"Aye," he said. "Gan on. Show him me legs, son."

And Slog knelt at his feet and rolled the bloke's tattered trouser bottoms up and showed the bloke's dirty socks and dirty shins.

"See?" he whispered.

He touched the bloke's legs with his fingers.

"Aren't they lovely?" he said. "Touch them, Davie."

I didn't move.

"Gan on," said the bloke. "Touch them, Davie."

His voice got colder.

"Do it for Slogger, Davie," he said.

I crouched, I touched, I felt the hair and the skin and the bones and muscles underneath. I recoiled. I stood up again.

"It's true, see?" said Slog. "He got them back in Heaven."

"What d'you think of that, then, Davie?" said the bloke.

Slog smiled.

"He thinks they're bliddy lovely, Dad."

Slog stroked the bloke's legs one more time, then rolled the trousers down again.

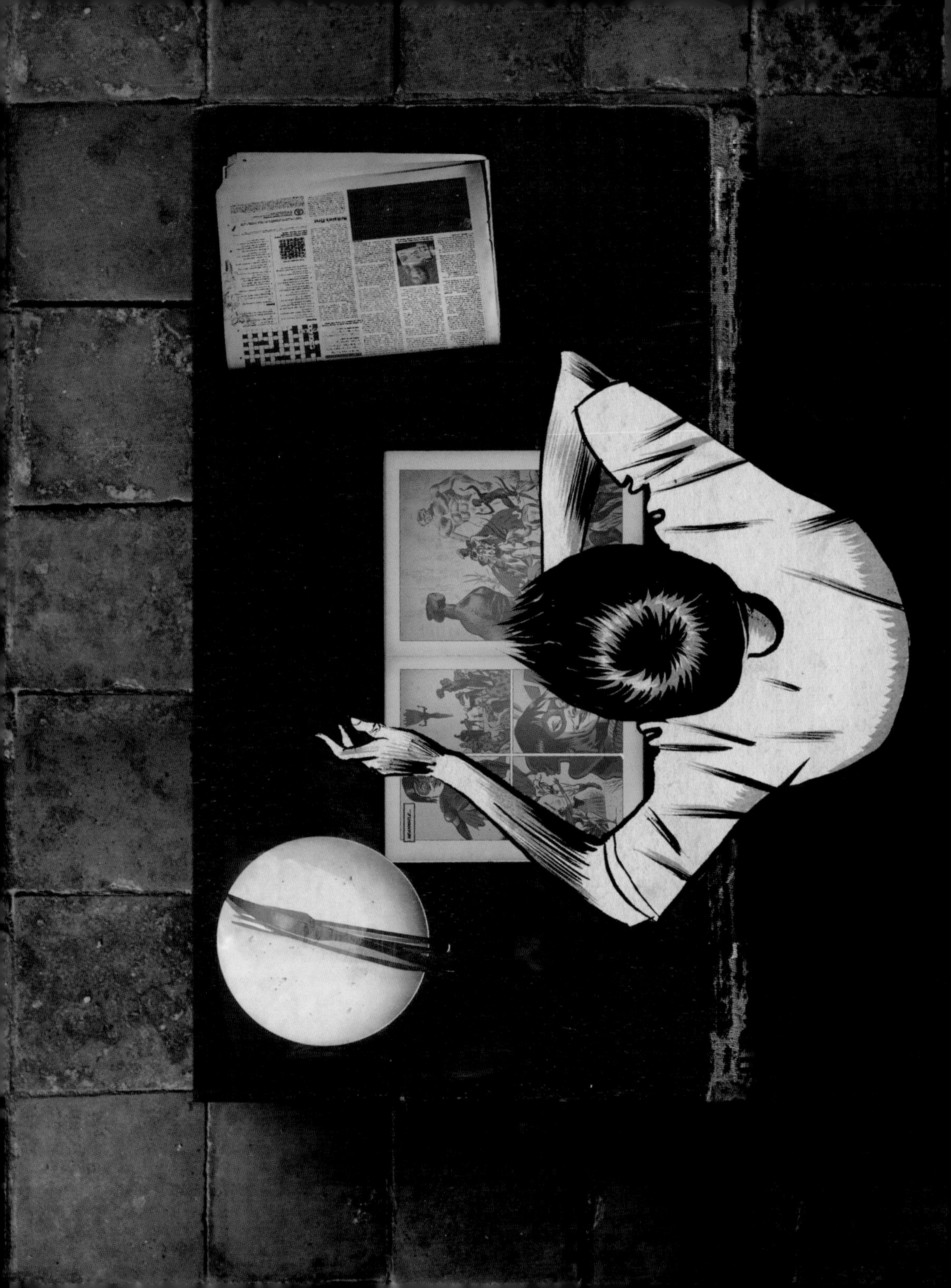

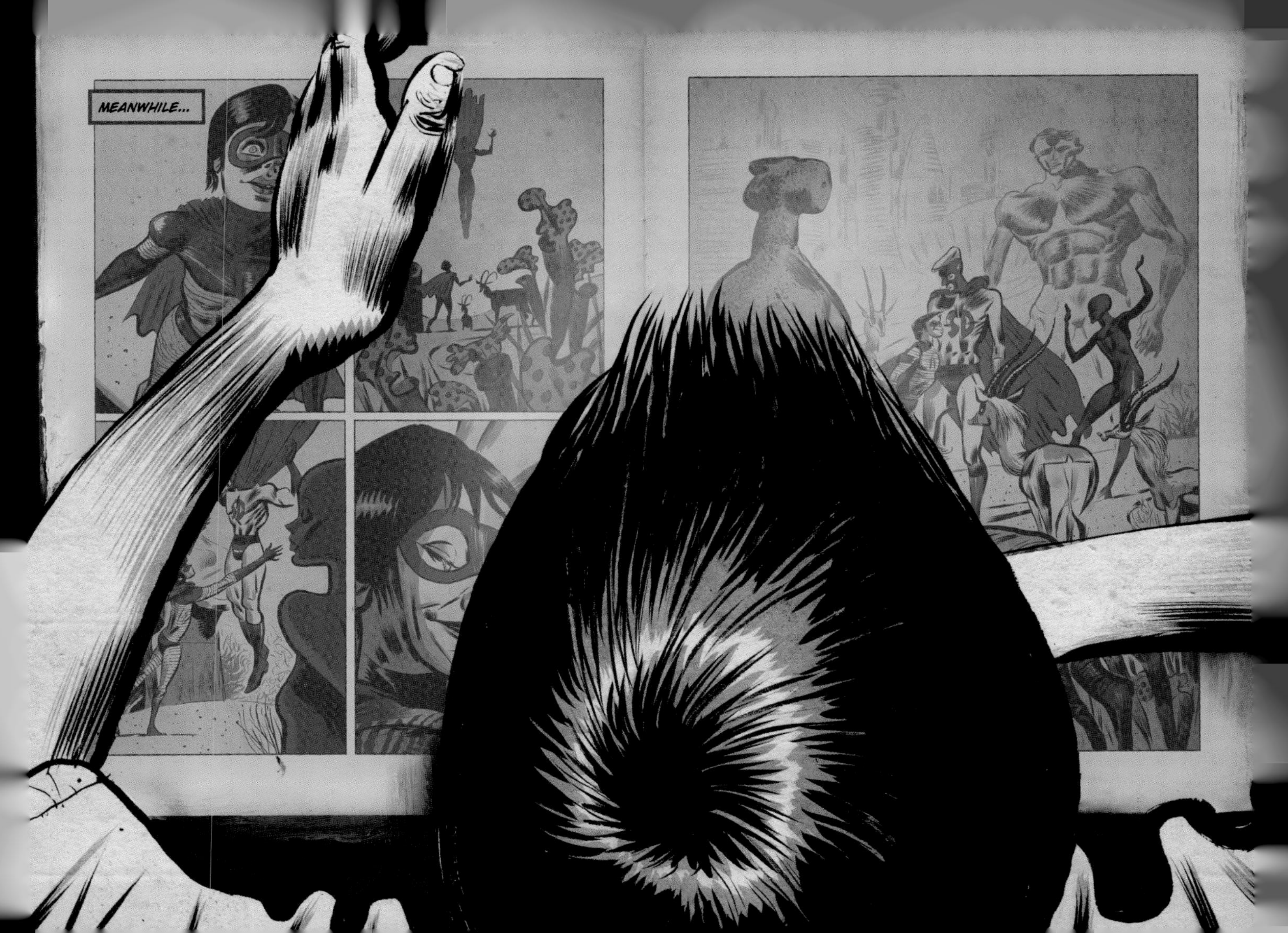
MEANWHILE...

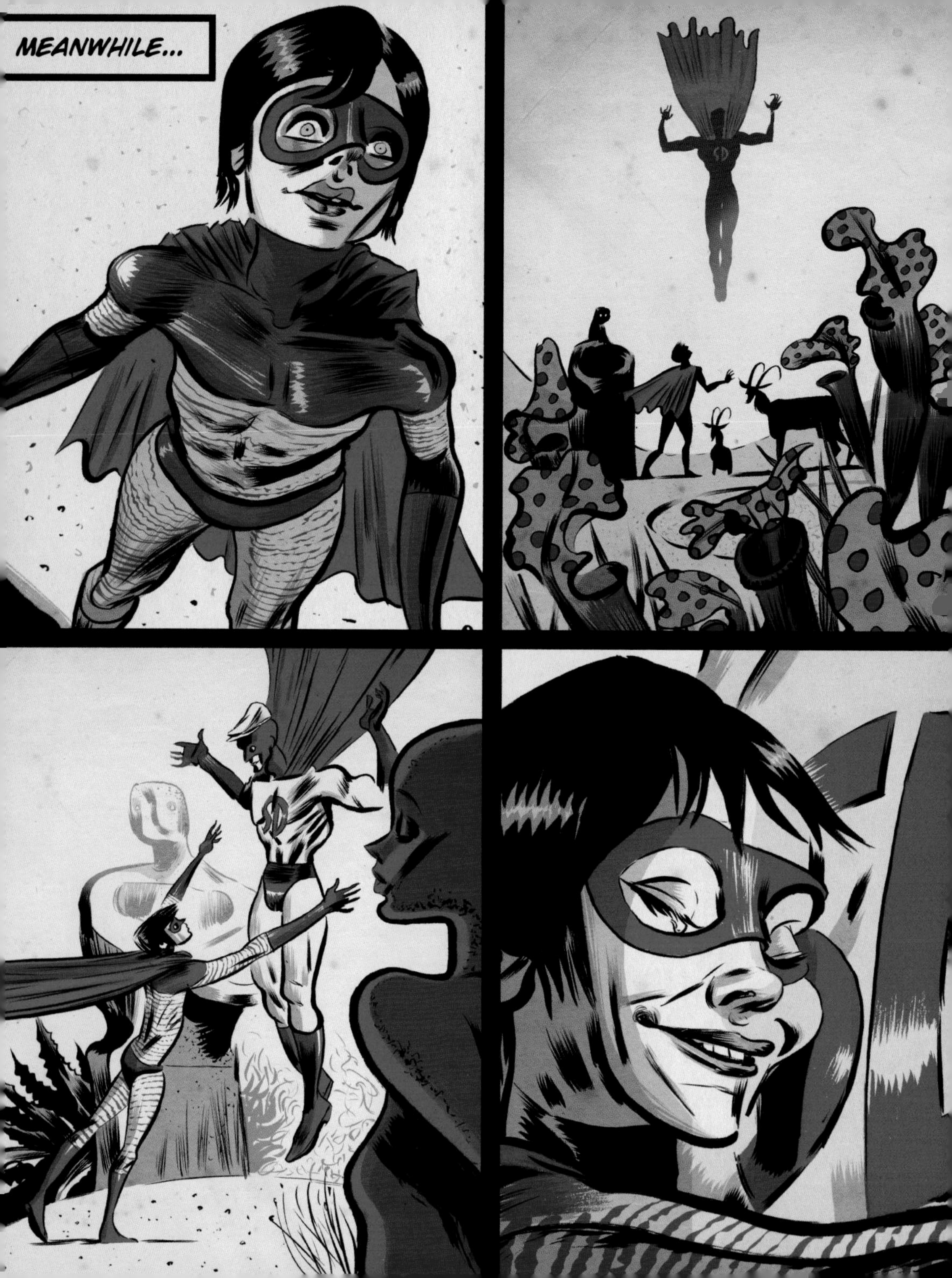
MEANWHILE...

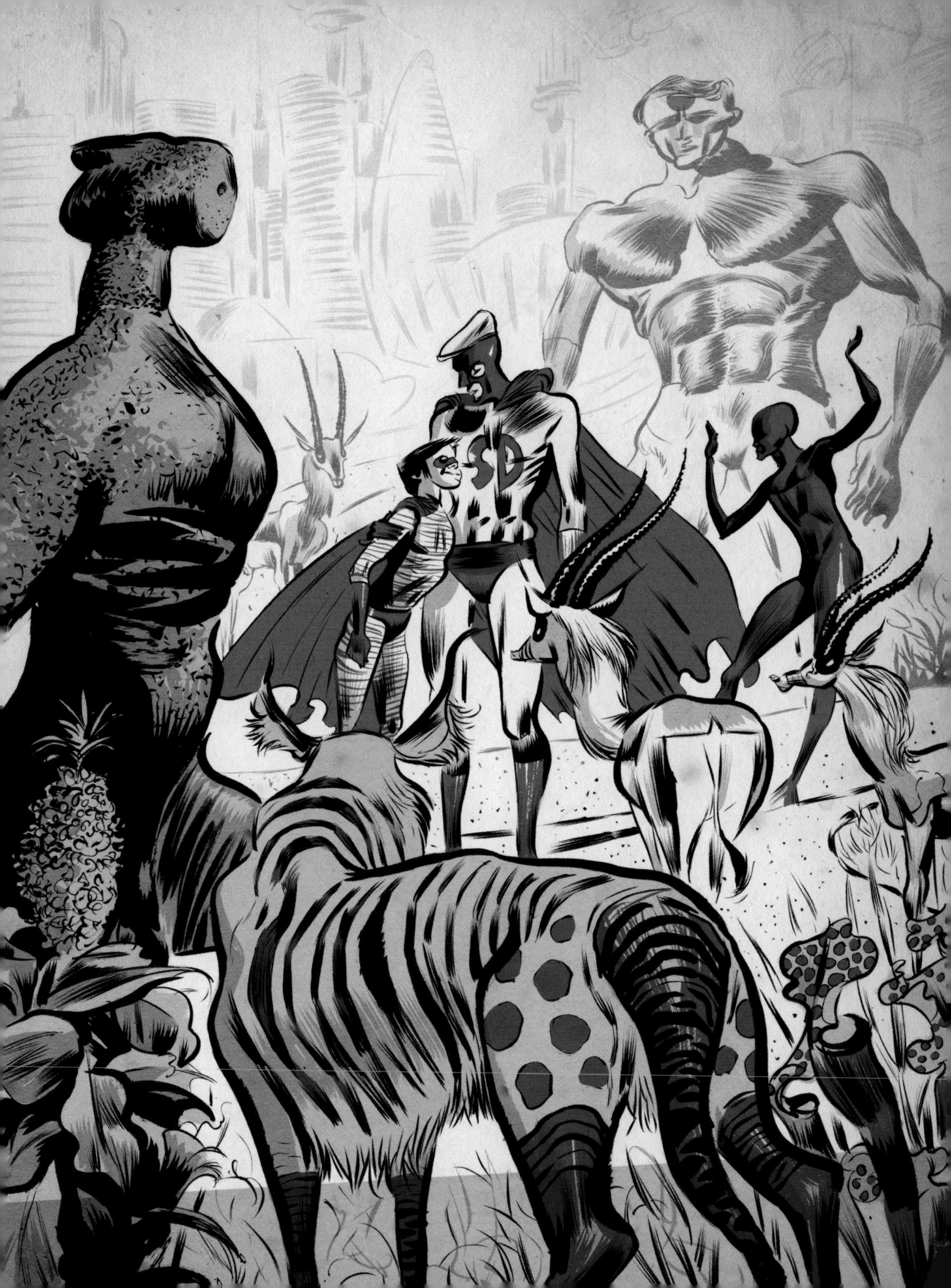

"What's Heaven like, Dad?" said Slog.

"Hard to describe, son."

"Please, Dad."

"It's like bright and peaceful and there's God and the angels and all that. . . ." The bloke looked at his sandwich. "It's like having all the saveloy dips you ever want. With everything, every time."

"It must be great."

"Oh, aye, son. It's dead canny."

"Are you coming to see Mam, Dad?" he said.

The bloke pursed his lips and sucked in air and gazed into the sky.

"Dunno. Dunno if I've got the time, son."

Slog's face fell.

The bloke reached out and stroked Slog's cheek.

"This is very special," he said. "Very rare. They let it happen cos you're a very rare and special lad."

He looked into the sky and talked into the sky.

"How much longer have I got?" he said, then he nodded. "Aye. OK. OK."

He shrugged and looked back at Slog.

"No," he said. "Time's pressing. I cannot do it, son."

There were tears in Slog's eyes.

"She misses you that much, Dad," he said.

"Aye. I know." The bloke looked into the sky again. "How much longer?" he said.

He took Slog in his arms.

"Come here," he whispered.

I watched them hold each other tight.

"You can tell her about me," said the bloke. "You can tell her I love and miss her and all." He looked at me over Slog's shoulder. "And so can Davie, your best mate. Can't you, Davie? Can't you?"

"Aye," I muttered.

[illegible] England football team finished their season, eventually, by beating Kazakhstan and Andorra. Not exactly mind-blowing, I know, bu[t] us not sneer. England were requ[ired] to be flat track bullies and they played the part to perfection. It w[as] not always thus.

It's a rum thing to be asked to [do] when you think about it. A team [or] an individual can be one of the b[est] in the world and they are asked t[o] play against somebody who coul[d] never even dream of such a thing. And accomplishing this task is by [no] means straightforward.

There is a tendency to let them [off] from tender-heartedness. There is [a] tendency not to compete too hard because you can't get your blood [up]. And there is the point that the opposition are not really trying to beat you, they are just trying to g[ive] you a bad time. And these are no[t] the problems you are accustomed [to] dealing with.

These occasions are … perhaps particularly to an English person just plain embarrassing. You don't want to play them and, when forc[ed] to, you just want to get them over with as quickly as possible, and somehow to do so without lookin[g a] fool.

Footballers are asked to do this quite often, in domestic cup competitions, in qualification tournaments and in the group sta[ges] of tournament finals. In rugby un[ion] it happens sometimes. In tennis, t[he] early rounds are full of mismatche[s].

Why, England football followers have always asked, are the Germa[ns] so good at being flat track bullies and the English so bad? And shou[ld] we plume ourselves on this failing [or] repose in it?

But over the past ten months, w[ith] seven wins from seven World Cup qualifiers, England have at last embraced the role of flat-track bullies unembarrassed and really rather unlikeable. It is nothing less than a triumph and certainly Fabio Capello's greatest achievement so [far] as England manager.

Francis Elliott Deputy Political Editor

George Osborne confirms for the first time today that he would make significant cuts in public spending and says that Labour is being "dishonest" about the action required to avert financial disaster.

The Shadow Chancellor, writing in *The Times*, admits that, until now, he has "tip-toed" around the need for cuts, but says he believes that voters are ready to reward honesty.

He accuses Gordon Brown of masking Labour's own plans to cut spending after the next election and suggests that even cuts of 10 per cent in all departments but health and overseas aid may not be be enough to shore up Britain's credibility on the international money markets.

Andrew Lansley, the party's health spokesman, caused controversy last week when he spoke of cuts of 10 per cent for other departments because of David Cameron's commitment to real terms rises in health budgets despite falling overall spending.

Mr Brown seized on the remark, claiming he had revealed a "cuts plan that is wide, deep and immediate".

But Mr Osborne confirms that a Tory government would, indeed, cut spending, in an attempt to reshape the public debate. "We Conservatives, like Labour politicians, have fought shy of using the 'c' word … cuts. We've all been tip-toeing around one of those discredited Gordon Brown dividing lines for too long … The real dividing line is not 'cut versus investment' but honesty versus dishonest," Mr Osborne writes.

"We should have the confidence to tell the public the truth that Britain faces a debt crisis, that real spending will have to be cut, whoever is elected, and that the bills of rising unemployment and the huge interest costs of a soaring national debt means that many government departments will face cuts in their budgets. These are statements of fact and to deny them invites ridicule."

Despite Mr Osborne's plea for honesty about the need for cuts, he gives no specific Conservative spending plans, saying only that he will set out "more details in due course". The party has given some indications, however, including the intention to scrap ID cards. Nor does he commit the party to declaring its plans before the election. "Some savings will only become apparent when we have the chance to look at the books in government," he writes.

Mr Osborne refers to himself, members of his Treasury team and other Shadow Cabinet members attending a meeting of Canadian ministers who described how they were able to cut spending in the 1990s. The Canadian government at that time cut spending by 10 per cent and reduced its deficit to 3 per cent of GDP in two years, cutting budgets for hospitals, schools and universities, unemployment and defence.

Meanwhile, Kenneth Clarke, the Shadow Business Secretary, threatened more Tory division on Europe by suggesting that Mr Cameron would not seek to reopen negotiations on the Lisbon treaty if it had been [been] ratified by the time he came to power.

Mr Clarke angered Tory Eurosceptics by saying he envisaged only "sensible discussions … in limited areas about the division of responsibilities

The Shadow Chancellor does not specify cuts but ID cards would go

[illegible]

The next step for the Tories is to provide detail on how they intend to reduce spending

[illegible]

It's ridiculous to pretend there won't be cuts

[illegible]

[illegible], whips off the bails to stump Yuvraj [illegible], as India's run chase falls short

enough overs from his second line of attack. Yuvraj drove his first ball over long on and soon hit a second six against Graeme Swann, but the spin bowler gained revenge when he coaxed Yuvraj slightly out of his crease to drive, beat the edge and saw James Foster complete a smart stumping.

Yusuf Pathan took up the challenge, scoring from every one of the 17 deliveries faced. At the other end, Mahendra Singh Dhoni finally discovered a semblance of timing in a difficult tournament. In the context, Broad did well to restrict the sixth wicket pair to nine from the penultimate over. But, despite a six by Pathan against Sidebottom, the last ball four was a cause for commiseration not celebration for India.

England were entitled to feel all along that their own score was just about par: previous first innings on the same pitch had realised 150, 153 and 144. Once again, boundaries flowed sparsely from their bats … even Ireland hit more earlier in the day … and at times they overcomplicated with reverse shots. But they tore like hares between the wickets.

Pietersen, as always, stood in a class of his own. His early off drive against R. P. Singh was never bettered and he dealt easily with Yuvraj, his tormentor of yore. Bopara chipped in at a run a ball and the promotion of Dimitri Mascarenhas was not a failure as such. He just did not see the strike he wanted in the last five overs.

England were so elated at the result that Sidebottom, the man of the match for his first overs rather than his expensive last, said that the players would be cracking open the beers to celebrate. In the excitement, it had clearly not registered that they need to do the same again today. The fitness coaches may not approve.

Britain's first

England's triumph paves the way for a possible semi-final against Australia. Bouncing back from a nine-wicket defeat by New Zealand, Australia beat West Indies by eight wickets thanks to a breezy 58 by Shelley Nitschke. However, they had to hold their nerve after Deandra Dottin, the West Indies opener, made a fifty off 22 balls to record the fastest half-century in this format and help to set a competitive target of 136.

Across

1 Sorting out theft, lawman short of a stand-by (7,1)
7 I have bad habits, and incline to scratch (4)
9 Grass all the rage in the past (8)
10 Five in the morning, and quiet editor is seduced (6)
11 Gruesome globe put in, in the middle of … (6)
13 … models of solar system — be errors get made (8)
14 Stepper under the weather provide easy progress (5,7)
17 Having eaten fast, I give approval to mumbo jumbo (12)
20 Assumed diamonds to be shelved (3,2,3)
21 Pleasure boat limped along to some extent (6)
22 Alloy of gold originally making ornaments look unique (6)
23 Various patterns appear in part of church (8)
25 Rugby player has [illegible] (4)
26 Demand money at first during brief experience as a slave driver (10)

Down

2 Playfully, require nothing but … (8)
3 … convenience in game (3)
4 Shrinking cotton fabric shrunk up (5)
5 Polo taken to Northern Ireland by inventor (7)
6 Don't concern yourself with Edward, the rat catcher (5,4)
7 Ending in debt, Roger and Madge, distraught, borrowed more money (11)
8 More devoted person mourning (6)
12 Took robbing badly, delivering reprimand (5,2,4)
15 Another name is therefore given to fuel (9)
16 Two passes, and fold (8)
18 Upbringing fixed genuine character in Hamlet (7)
19 Measure round book (6)
21 Something of David's secreted initially in one's hand (5)
24 One interesting the police in class regularly (3)

Prize solution 24,245

Check today's answers by ringing 0906 7577100 by midnight. Calls cost 75p per minute

The winners of Prize Crossword No 24,245 are: Callum Daddy, London; Ceri Oxholmsten, Cardiff; [illegible] John Baron, Northumberland (online) [illegible] Wreath, Essex; Jeff Perry, Portugal (online)

[illegible]

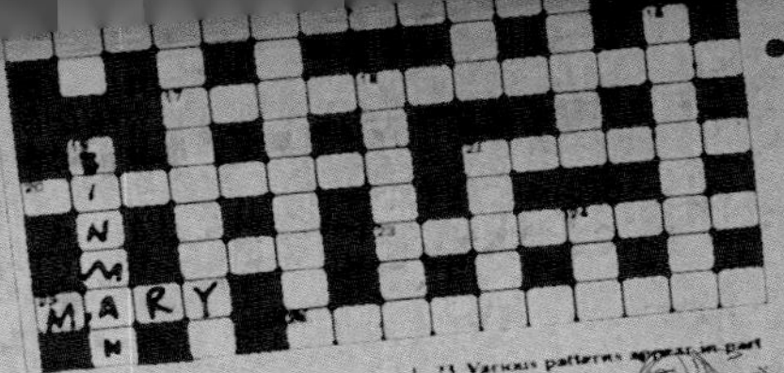

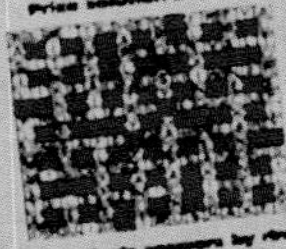

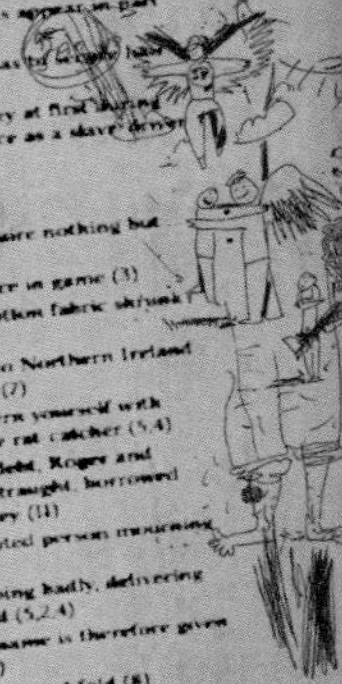

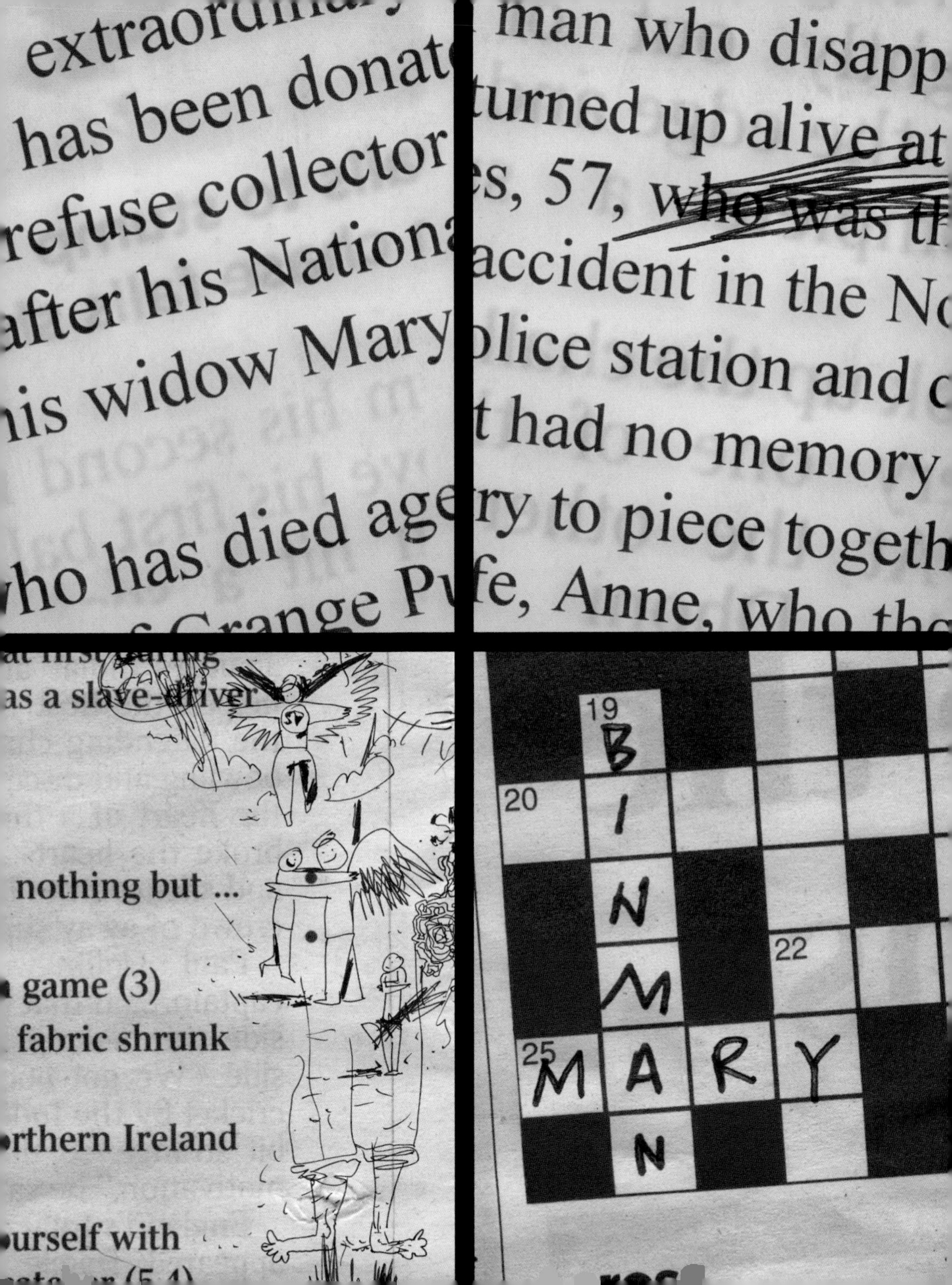
extraordi
has been donat
refuse collector
after his Nationa
his widow Mary
who has died age
Grange Pu
man who disapp
turned up alive at
es, 57, who was th
accident in the No
olice station and
t had no memory
ry to piece togeth
fe, Anne, who th
as a slave-driver
nothing but ...
game (3)
fabric shrunk
rthern Ireland
urself with
19 B
20 I
N
M
22
25 MARY
N

Then the bloke stood up. Slog still clung to him.

"Can I come with you, Dad?" he said.

The bloke smiled.

"You know you can't, son."

"What did you do?" I said.

"Eh?" said the bloke.

"What job did you do?"

The bloke looked at me, dead cold.

"I was a binman, Davie," he said. "I used to stink but I didn't mind. And I followed the stink to get me here."

He cupped Slog's face in his hands.

"Isn't that right, son?"

"Aye," said Slog.

"So what's Slog's mother called?" I said.

"Eh?"

"Your wife. What's her name?"

The bloke looked at me. He looked at Slog. He pushed the last bit of sandwich into his mouth and chewed. A sparrow hopped close to our feet, trying to get at the crumbs. The bloke licked his lips, wiped his chin, stared into the sky.

"Please, Dad," whispered Slog.

The bloke shrugged. He gritted his teeth and sighed and looked at me so cold and at Slog so gentle.

"Slog's mother," he said. "My wife . . ." He shrugged again. "She's called Mary."

"Oh, Dad!" said Slog, and his face was transfigured by joy. "Oh, Dad!"

The bloke laughed.

"Ha! Bliddy ha!"

He held Slog by the shoulders.

"Now, son," he said. "You got to stand here and watch me go and you mustn't follow."

"I won't, Dad," whispered Slog.

"And you must always remember me."

"I will, Dad."

"And me, you, and your lovely mam'll be together again one day in Heaven."

"I know that, Dad. I love you, Dad."

"And I love you."

And the bloke kissed Slog, and twisted his face at me, then turned away. He started singing "Faith of Our Fathers." He walked across the square past Myers' pork shop, and turned down onto the High Street. We ran after him then and we looked down the High Street past the people and the cars but there was no sign of him, and there never would be again.

We stood there speechless. Billy Myers came to the doorway of the pork shop with a bucket of bones in his hand and watched us.

"That was me dad," said Slog.

"Aye?" said Billy.

"Aye. He come back, like he said he would, in the spring."

"That's good," said Billy. "Come and have a dip, son. With everything."

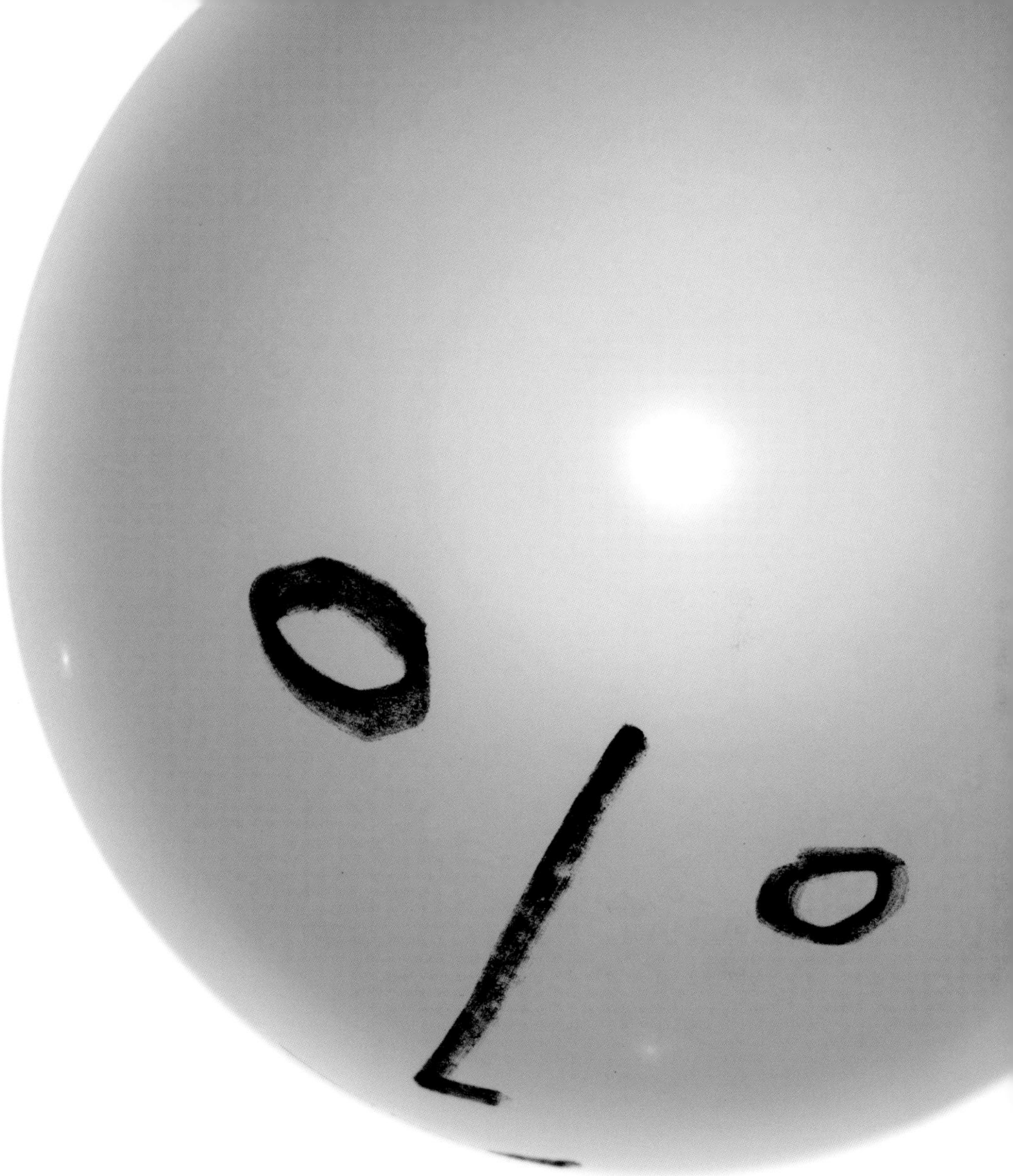

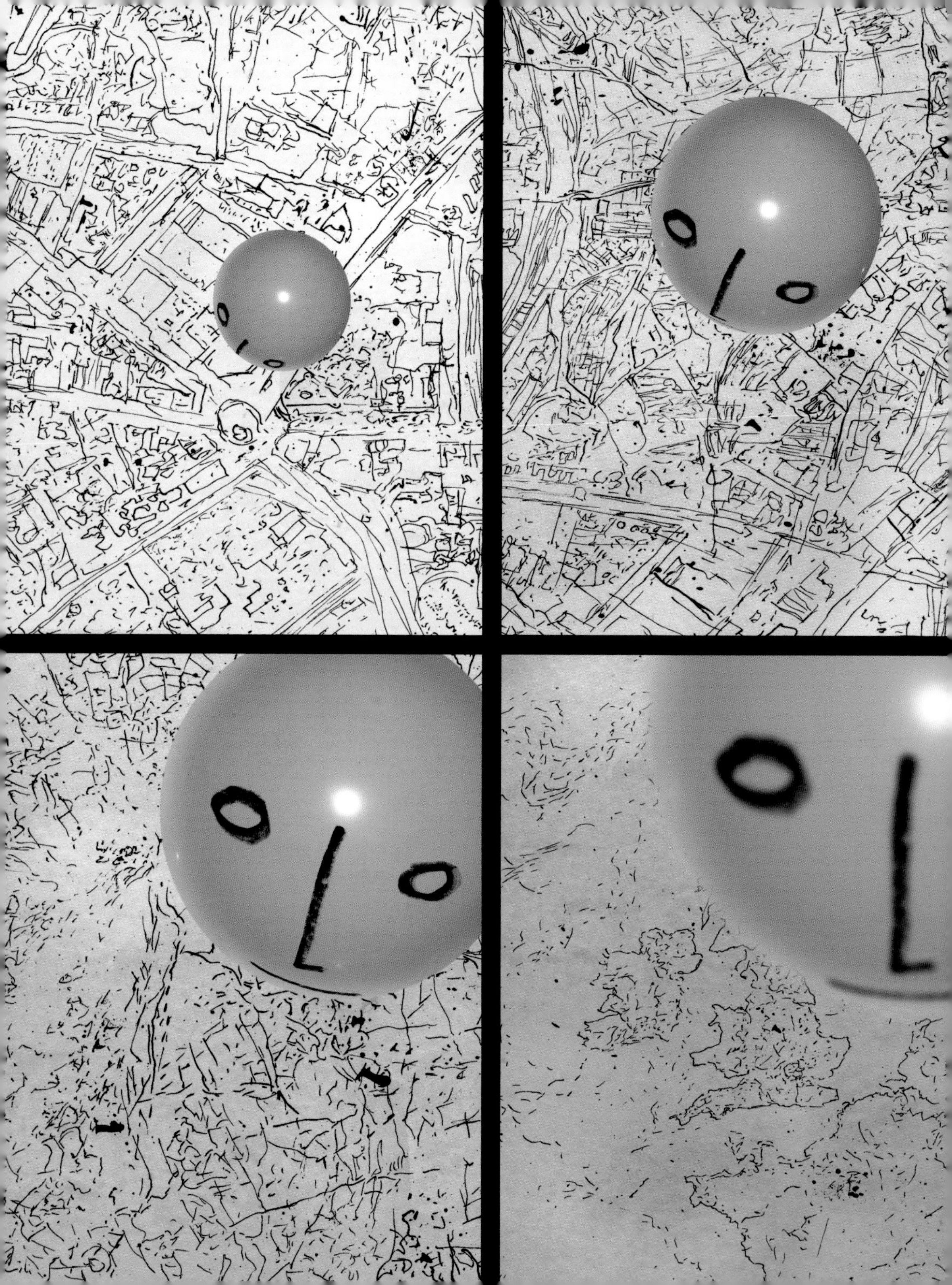

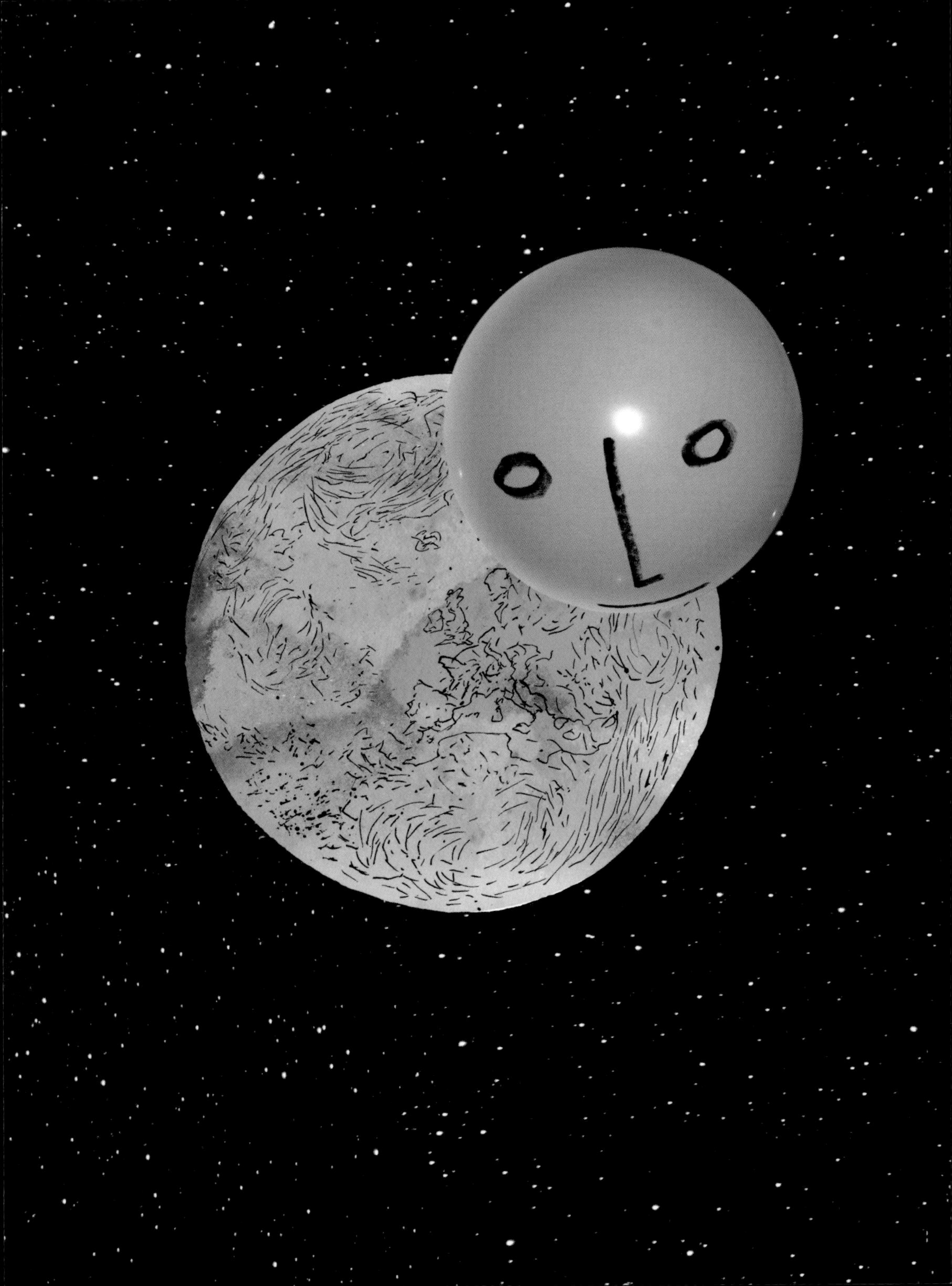

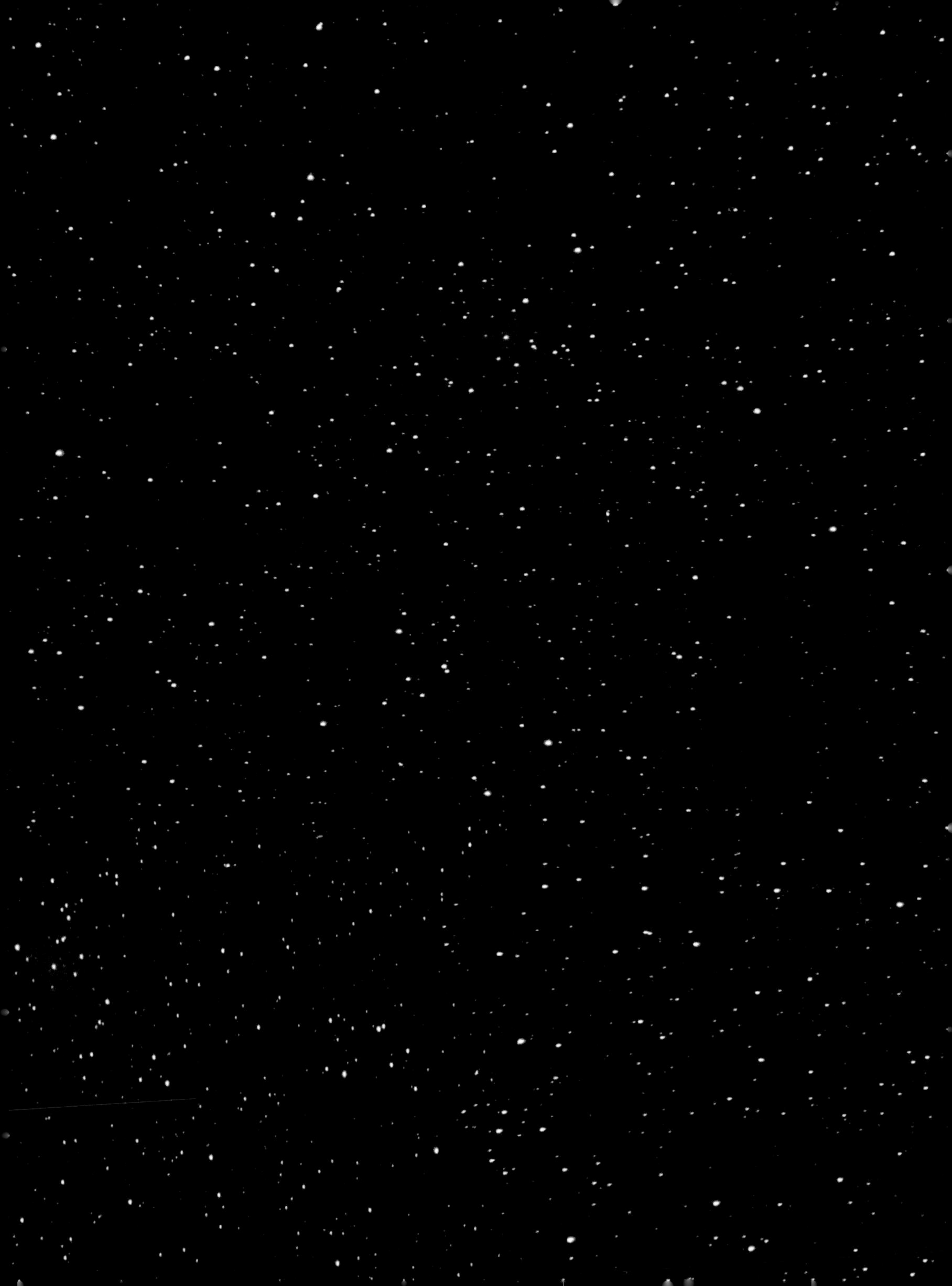

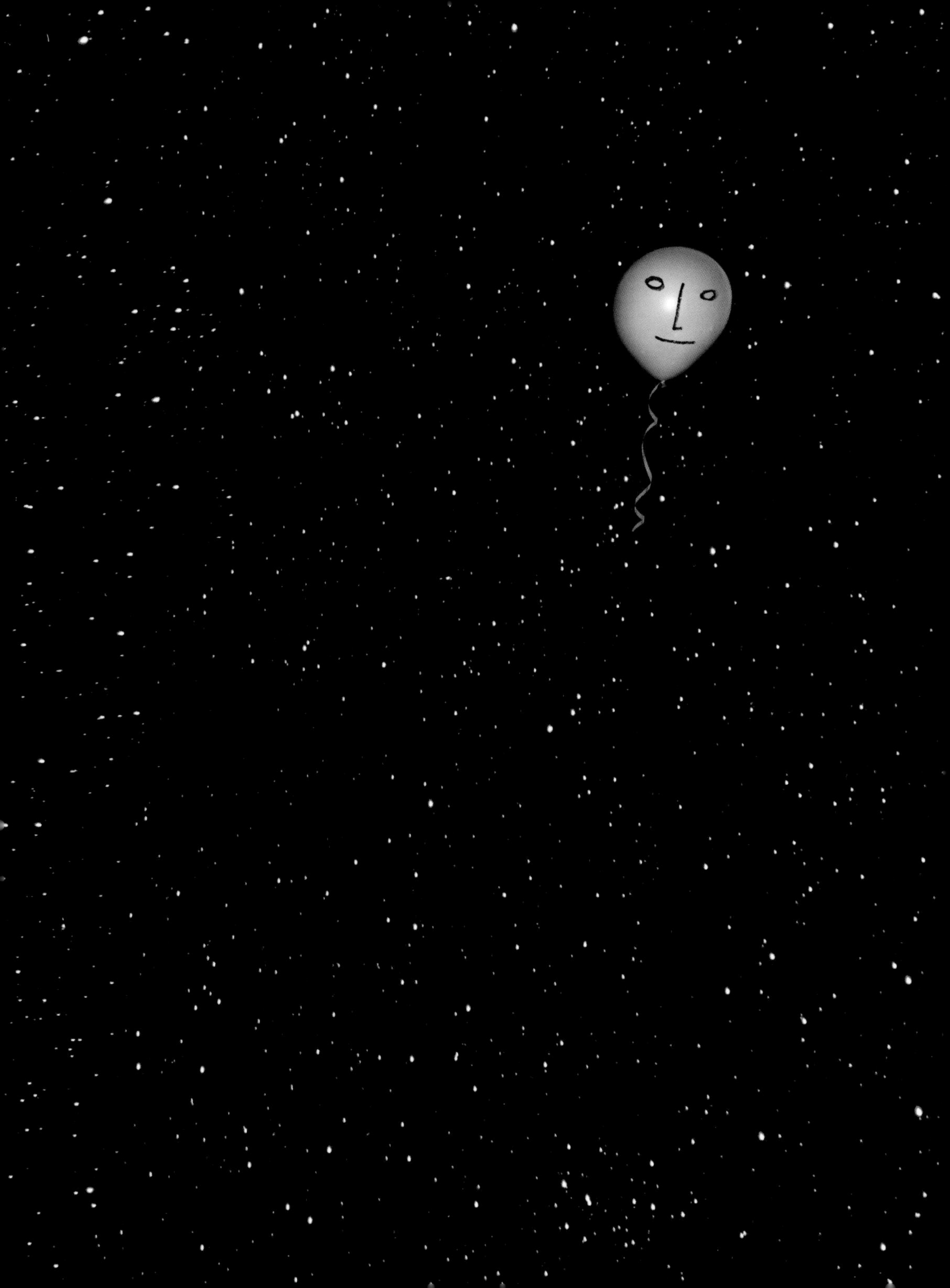

Slog's Dad was first commissioned as a short story by New Writing North and published in *So What Kept You?* (Flambard Press, 2006), then was runner-up in the 2007 National Short Story Prize, which led to its being published in *The National Short Story Prize* anthology (Atlantic Books, 2007), in *Prospect* magazine, and broadcast on BBC Radio 4.

First U.S. edition 2011

Library of Congress Cataloging-in-Publication Data is available.

Library of Congress Catalog Card Number pending

ISBN 978-0-7636-4940-1

10 11 12 13 14 15 16 17 CCP 10 9 8 7 6 5 4 3 2 1

Printed in Shenzhen, Guangdong, China

This book was typeset in Priori Sans.
The illustrations were done in ink and Photoshop.

Candlewick Press
99 Dover Street
Somerville, Massachusetts 02144

visit us at www.candlewick.com